PLAY IT COOL

(A Joe Sheldon Novel)

GREGORY
PAYETTE

Play It Cool

ISBN-13: 978-1-7361465-5-2
Published by 8 Flags Publishing, Inc.

Cover Design: James at GoOnWrite.com

Editing/Proofreading: Paula

paulaproofreader.wixsite.com and Terry

editerry.wixsite.com/proofreader

For Mary-Jane

Join My Reader's List

I'd like to invite you to join my reader list to receive free stories, giveaways, and VIP announcements when my new books are released. When you do, you'll receive two free books, *Tell Them I'm Dead* and *What Have You Done?*

Visit **GregoryPayette.com/free-book** to sign up now.

1

JOE HAD ALREADY had a long day. Boring, he'd say, with half of it spent wandering around the area just outside Ray's Auto Repair. He was told it would be one hour, but it'd already been over three. Which meant he'd had enough time to walk a mile for a coffee, stop in a Home Depot for no reason at all, and sit on a bench and stare at his phone until the battery hit 10 percent.

He'd brought his computer with him and took it out at the coffee shop but couldn't get his brain to do the work. He had one article to write before the deadline but knew he'd pull it off at the last minute, the way he'd always done it.

But what made it even harder was the stress of not knowing what kind of dent the repair bill would put in his wallet. It made it hard to think. His days of making a decent living writing for a big paper were behind him. The real newspaper jobs were hard to come by or didn't pay what they used to.

Joe stood in the parking lot and looked up from his phone when Colt called his name.

Colt was Dickie Caldwell's mechanic.

Dickie owned Ray's Auto Repair. He bought it—or more likely took it—off a guy named Ray who owed Dickie some money after making some ill-advised bets.

Colt pointed for Joe to meet him inside, then turned around and disappeared somewhere inside the garage.

Joe walked through the glass door with the sign taped to it that said, in faded black marker, *Customer entrance. No customers allowed inside garage.*

The waiting area inside was small and narrow with dark brown paneling on the walls. Three chairs Joe remembered from Dickie's kitchen were pushed together across from the service counter. The smell of burnt coffee and exhaust filled the air.

Colt had his back to Joe and poured a cup of coffee from the carafe, stained brown, top to bottom. Joe had tried a cup three hours earlier and dumped it as soon as he walked outside. He wasn't sure how anyone could drink it but figured it out when Colt poured half the glass jar of sugar into his Styrofoam cup. He stirred it with a plastic stirrer and took a sip, glanced over the rim at Joe and said, "Sorry it took so long." He took another sip. "But you're not going to like what I found."

Joe turned and glanced at an attractive younger

woman seated at a desk in a small office on the far end of the service area, past the other end of the counter. She looked back at Joe through the doorway and smiled. He gave her a nod and turned back to Colt. "So what's the story?"

"The story is your timing belt is shot; your radiator has a leak; you need a new thermostat… and I can't say for sure, but your water pump might be bad… which is likely what brought you here in the first place. We change the timing belt, we'd have to do the water pump anyway."

"What am I looking at?"

"You mean how much?" Colt nodded toward the office at the other end of the customer service area, where the young woman sat behind the desk. "I think she's typing up the estimate for you, but if I had to guess, you're looking at a couple grand… parts and labor."

"I can't drive it the way it is?" Joe said.

Colt shook his head. "I don't think so."

Joe looked at the clock on the wall. "Okay. I'll have to think about it. Don't do anything yet."

"I won't be working on it tonight anyway. We close in half an hour."

"I'll call you in the morning," Joe said. "I'll let you know what I decide."

Colt walked out into the garage and Joe stared into the work area at his car. He pulled out his phone to see who he could call for a ride, but by that point his phone was dead. He glanced into the small office with the woman at the desk. She was pretty, from what he could see. Long blonde hair and young. Maybe in her twenties. "Excuse me," he said.

She looked up from her work. "Oh, hi. Can I help you with something?"

"Yeah, I, uh… just wondering if Dickie's around?"

She shook her head. "Sorry, no. Not until morning. He told me to get him up early, so…"

Joe didn't know what she meant by that. Maybe he paid the woman to wake him up, part of her job. She couldn't have been one of his kids. They'd all moved out and moved away. And they were older than her, he thought.

He stepped to the office and stood in the doorway. "You mind if I use your phone?" He held his phone up to show her. "Battery's dead."

She stared back at him with her blue eyes, then lifted the cordless phone from the receiver. She rolled her chair back from the desk. "Do you want me to give you some privacy?"

"No, please. Stay right there," he said. He kept his eyes on her, then stepped out into the waiting area. He called his friend Will, who he'd known from his days at the *Post*.

But Will didn't answer, and Joe didn't bother to leave a message. He stepped back into the office and handed the woman the phone. He looked out the office window and to the edge of the parking lot along the street. "Is that a bus stop out front?"

She turned in her chair and glanced out in the same direction, then turned to Joe. "Do you need a ride? If you can give me twenty minutes, I can give you a lift."

He hesitated. "If it's not too much trouble. I don't want to put you out."

She smiled, close to a smirk. "I assume you live in Miami?"

"Just over the bridge. I could actually walk if—"

"Give me twenty minutes. Wait out there and I'll finish up." Her eyes were on the paper in front of her. "You own the Taurus?"

"Yeah, that's mine."

She held the paper up in front of him. "I was going to work on your estimate before I left. But Dickie'll take a look at it in the morning."

They both held a gaze on each other.

"I'll get out of your way so you can finish up," Joe said.

He turned from the doorway and went over to the waiting area with the old kitchen chairs. He sat and leaned forward just enough so he could look in through the doorway.

Her eyes were on the paperwork in front of her. She had a pen in her hand, and he noticed a diamond ring on her finger. But it was on her right hand. He had no idea what that could've meant. Maybe she was divorced, didn't want to give up the jewelry.

She looked up from the desk and caught him staring at her. "I'm Scarlett, by the way."

He got up, walked back to her office and stood in the doorway. "Nice to meet you, Scarlett. Pretty name." He smiled. "I'm Joe. Joe Sheldon."

She gave him a bright smile. She had very white teeth. "I know who you are." She held up the piece of paper in front of her.

"Oh, right. The estimate."

She stared up at him. "Are you the writer from the *Post?*"

Joe didn't even tell many people he was a writer. Not anymore. He felt more like a fraud. "I used to be."

Joe pulled open the passenger door and ducked inside the vintage yellow Mercedes. He was familiar with the model and knew it had the diesel engine. The leather seats were cracked, and it had the original AM/FM cassette player. "This an eighty-five?" he said.

Scarlett slid the key in the ignition and turned over the engine. She shrugged. "All I know is it's old. Dickie thought I'd like it, for some reason."

"You don't?"

She turned to him without an answer. "Where're we going?"

"Where do you want to go?" But as soon as it left his lips, he felt like a fool.

She had her eyes in the rearview, backed from the parking space and maneuvered the old Mercedes through the parking lot. The spacing was tight, with all the cars parked outside. Some had For Sale signs; others looked like they'd have to be towed away. The rest fell somewhere in between.

"Busy place," Joe said.

She nodded. "It is. Nonstop. And it's just Colt right now. Dickie said he could use another mechanic, but he doesn't want to pay what most guys want." She pulled the car to the edge of the lot and edged the nose of the Mercedes closer to the busy street.

It was rush hour. The cars buzzed by in both directions.

"I hate trying to pull out of here," Scarlett said. She turned her head left and right along the street.

Joe realized he hadn't told her which way to go.

"Like I said, I'm right over the bridge. But that's to the left. And it doesn't look like we'll get out of here anytime soon going that way. So if you take a right…"

She turned to him. "You're not in a hurry to get home?"

Joe shook his head but kept his eyes out on the street. "Not if it means getting killed trying to get out of here."

She watched to her left, then slammed her foot on the pedal and ripped the car out into traffic going right. She nearly cut off an oncoming car.

Joe watched her. He liked her looks. But he knew she was much younger than him. Or at least she looked it. And then there was the ring.

"Car's got some power," he said. "It's a 330D with the turbo diesel, right?" He ran his hand over the dash. "I like the older ones like this."

Scarlett gave him a quick glance. "I don't have a choice, living with a man who owns a repair shop."

Joe wasn't sure he heard her right. But then thought it made sense after what she'd said earlier about getting him up early.

But Dickie was somewhere in his sixties. Upper, he thought. He tried to look at her without being creepy.

As soon as he did, Scarlett turned to him. "Do you want to grab a drink?"

2

JOE STOOD IN front of Scarlett outside his apartment door and dug his hand into his pocket. He pulled out his key, slid it into the lock and pushed the door open. He extended his arm toward the open doorway. "After you."

Scarlett walked in ahead of him and turned to Joe behind her.

Joe looked toward the clock up on the wall. He didn't have much time to submit his article. "One drink, then I have to get to work."

He opened the cabinet door in the kitchen and pulled out a bottle of Smirnoff and two glasses. He reached into the refrigerator and pushed aside the old containers of Chinese food and reached for the cranberry juice. He made two drinks and reached back inside the refrigerator, took out two pieces of lime he'd already cut earlier and dropped one into each drink. He handed her a glass and raised his in a toast.

The wall at the right of the adjoining room was lined with wooden shelves Joe made himself with planks and cinder blocks. The shelves held his extensive collection of record albums.

Scarlett's eyes went wide as she walked into the room. "I guess you collect records?" She looked back at him but he didn't have to answer. She sipped her drink and reached for an album, looked at the cover, flipped it over, and glanced at the back. She slid the record onto the shelf and ran her eyes along Joe's collection. "Is there anything you don't have?" she said.

Joe stepped toward her. "There's plenty I don't have." He knew where everything was, organized in alphabetical order. He pulled out Levon Helm's final album, *Dirt Farmer*. He removed it from the sleeve, held it with his fingers on the edges, and placed it on the turntable sitting on top of his homemade shelves. He clicked a button on the front of the player and the title song, "Poor Old Dirt Farmer" came on over the speakers—the old kind with the wood grain on the sides and foam speaker grilles—in the two opposite corners of the room. He walked to the couch and sat with his drink. He just listened.

Scarlett fingered through the albums with her back to Joe.

"Can I ask you something?" he said.

She turned to him but didn't answer.

Joe was relaxed on the couch, one arm up on the

cushions and his leg crossed with his ankle over his knee. He rested his drink on his thigh. "When we were at the shop, you said something about waking Dickie up in the morning." Joe shrugged, then sipped his drink. He looked at her over the rim.

"He can't wake up with an alarm," she said. "Never hears it."

Joe thought for a moment. "Okay, but I guess I'm not clear. Why *you*?"

"Why *me*? Who else is going to wake him up?" She laughed. "I set my alarm, then roll over, and wake him up."

Joe almost choked on the sip he had just taken. A little vodka cranberry dribbled down his chin. "You... you and Dickie are—"

She nodded. "I thought you knew. I'm sorry, I guess I just assumed, since you and Dickie are friends, and—"

"No! Of course I don't know that. I wouldn't have..." He stopped, mid-sentence and turned, looked out the glass doors into the night sky. He was quiet. "Why didn't you tell me you and Dickie were together?"

Scarlett let out a slight laugh and walked to one of the two wingback chairs at the far end of the long room, between the record shelves and the glass doors. There was a small gas fireplace built into the wall. She sat and sipped her drink. "We have a special arrangement," she said. She crossed one leg over the other.

Joe looked back at her but stayed quiet. His eyes went to her long legs, but he looked away, then got up and walked to the stereo. "The Mountain" had started to play, but he lowered the volume. He faced the records but turned to his left and stared back at Scarlett. "I'm just being honest when I say this, but if I knew you and Dickie were together, I wouldn't have invited you up here."

"He doesn't mind I go out and have a good time."

He turned to the glass doors and looked out into the night, smiling. Under his breath, he said, "Goddamn, Dickie." He looked back at Scarlett. "How old are you? I'm guessing half his age?"

"Twenty-nine. But age is just a number, isn't it?" She got up from her chair and walked up to Joe. But she took her time, walked with one foot carefully placed in front of the other. Like she was on some kind of catwalk.

Joe didn't like it and tried to back up as she approached him.

She put her glass on one of the shelves with the albums.

But Joe grabbed it right away, walked past her and put it on the coffee table.

She turned and walked toward him. She reached for his arm and gave him a look that would normally get him in trouble. He knew he'd have to ask her to leave. His heart raced. Some of it was from the booze. But he couldn't deny she didn't look good, dressed casual in her shorts and a tank top, with her golden Florida tan. Her perfume was strong and he wasn't sure he'd noticed it much until then.

Jesus Christ.

She had her hand on his arm, but he pulled it away. He stepped back, away from her. "I'm sorry. Listen… Dickie's a friend of mine. He slipped past her and walked to the refrigerator, filled half his glass with vodka and topped it off with a few cubes and what little cranberry he had left. Not that another drink would help him think any clearer.

"So how long have you and Dickie, uh, been together?"

"Six months," she said.

Joe watched her take the last sip of her drink, but he wasn't going to offer her a refill. "That explains things," he said. "I don't think I've seen him in a few months. Might've been a year, since—"

"Do you know him from the shop?" She held out her glass before he answered. "Would you mind fixing me another drink?"

Joe shook his head. "I knew him before he bought it from Ray. Dickie and I go way back. Back when I was working for the *Post*. We used to help each other out."

He took her glass, leaned over and looked into the refrigerator. "I'm out of cranberry." He looked back over his shoulder. "You want tonic?"

"Just the vodka's fine. Maybe with a lime, if you have one?"

He fixed up her drink with a couple of cubes and a lime and handed the glass back to her.

There was a round table between them, the one he took from his mother's house after she died.

Scarlett raised her glass in a toast, then took a good sip. She looked at him over her glass, then turned, and walked across the room. She stopped at the wingback chair—the one from his aunt's house —next to the fireplace. She sat and looked across the room at Joe. "Are you a gambler, Joe?"

He walked out from the kitchen and stopped at the turntable. He pulled *Dirt Farmer* off the turntable and slid it back in the sleeve inside the album cover. He glanced at her. "A gambler? No." He looked at the clock on the wall above the shelves. "Why?"

She stared back at him but didn't answer. She had one leg crossed over the other and bounced her foot a bit.

He didn't like the silence. He never did, even when a strange woman wasn't in his apartment. "Something else you want to hear?"

Scarlett got up from her chair and stepped toward him. She reached into the middle shelf and grabbed the album she'd looked at earlier. "Can you play this?"

Joe took it from her and looked at the cover. "Blondie, huh?" He pulled the album from the sleeve, placed it on the player and turned the volume up a notch. He walked into the kitchen and grabbed his drink he had left on the table. He took a sip and leaned back against the front of the sink. "So, you sure Dickie doesn't care you're out this late?"

"A late night out to Dickie is nine thirty. And that's the weekend, with a good nap in the afternoon." She sipped her drink and emptied the glass, sucked on an ice cube.

Joe said, "I think maybe it'd be best you didn't tell him you were over here. I mean, it's not that anything's happened, but…"

"Oh, I already told him," she said. "I called him when we were at the bar, said I'd drop you off and maybe have a drink if you offered."

"You told him *that*? What'd he say?"

"That he'd be there in the morning to talk to you about your car."

3

JOE SAW DICKIE behind the desk when he walked in the shop, relieved it wasn't Scarlett back there in the small office. He was nervous, for no other reason than he couldn't help but wonder exactly what Scarlett might've told Dickie.

Dickie leaned way back in the big office chair, the phone against his ear and his eyes looking up toward the ceiling. He was heavier than Joe remembered, although he had always been on the stocky side. He was one of those guys who never tucked in his shirt, let it hang over to cover his round stomach. But he always kept himself looking good for a man his age, with his golden Florida tan and what little white hair he had on the sides of his head slicked back with hair product.

Joe knocked on the door's wooden frame.

Dickie looked at him and straightened out in his chair, gave Joe a wave and pointed to the chair against the wall next to the desk.

He put up his finger for Joe to wait and continued his call. "Hey, Rocco, just take care of your end of the deal and I'll take care of mine. Okay?" Dickie nodded into the phone. "Yeah, for your sake... I hope you do." He hung up and stood up from the desk, reached out and shook Joe's hand. "Hey, Joey. It's been a long time. Scarlett told me she was having a couple of drinks with you. I was jealous." He sat back in his chair. "I miss the old days, you and I having a few cocktails together." He leaned forward with his elbows on his desk, his hands folded together in front of his chin.

Joe sat in the chair and gave Dickie a quick couple of nods. "We'll have to do it again. You and me, I mean."

Dickie looked out the window into the lot. "Thanks for driving her home." He turned to Joe and smiled. "You like that Mercedes?"

"You know me. I appreciate the old things."

Dickie laughed. "You mean, like me?" He turned again to the window and looked toward the old Mercedes. "If you want it, you can have it. I know you wanted to keep your Ford running, but..." He picked up the piece of paper in front of him. "Looking at your estimate..."

"Isn't it Scarlett's?"

"The Mercedes? No. It's mine." He lowered his head and looked out through the doorway, then shifted his eyes back to Joe. His voice hushed, he said, "Client had a tough time covering a stupid bet. Just got my hands on it a couple of weeks ago. And besides, she wants something newer." He looked at the paper in his hand, then tossed it on the desk and leaned back in his chair. "She's a kid, you know? Give her another couple weeks, I can almost guarantee she'll put regular fuel in it, ruin the engine."

Joe felt uncomfortable. There was no doubt it was weird he was out having drinks with Dickie's girlfriend... had to force himself to drive her home before something stupid happened. "So I'm surprised you've never mentioned her," he said.

"Who? Scarlett? I met her at the Fuzzy Gull. I was alone at the bar and she came over, sat down next to me. The two of us ended up shooting the shit for a few hours." He shrugged. "We just connected. You know what I mean?" He looked into his Styrofoam cup. "She's beautiful, isn't she?"

Joe didn't answer.

Dickie took a sip from the cup, then made a face. "Christ, this coffee's not too good. It's for the customers. But I needed a boost, you know?" He stood up from his chair. "You wanna go grab a real coffee?"

"Yeah, I could use one. Just got done with an article before I came over here. I haven't slept yet."

"No shit, huh? Still working for that local rag?"

Joe got up and followed Dickie toward the glass door just past the coffee machine. "Pays the bills.

18

Most of them, at least."

They stepped into the garage and Dickie turned, looked at Joe over his shoulder. "Nothing like the big papers, huh?"

"I don't know how they make their money, to be honest. I wouldn't be surprised they cut me loose one of these days. They could get a kid, cover the same shit for a tenth my rate."

Dickie held the door for Joe. "What about your friend Will? He still in the same business? I heard he was doing security or something?"

"You could say that. He got his private investigator's license, was doing work for a small insurance company, shooting photos and video for their fraud division."

"No shit? No more newspaper photography?"

"I'm the only one who can't seem to let go... realize the industry'll just keep spinning around the drain for a few more years until it all ends for good." Joe spotted his Taurus in one of the bays. "What about my car?"

Dickie stopped and turned to Joe. "That's why I mentioned the Mercedes. It's time to put that piece of shit to bed. I saw the estimate Colt wrote up for you." Dickie shook his head. "I won't let you sink another penny into that thing. I know you like to drive 'em into the ground. I think you did a pretty good job of it." He continued again toward the open door at the back of the garage. "Time to pull the plug, Joey."

Dickie was the only one who called him Joey. Other than his mother and his aunts, who he hardly spoke to anymore. He didn't like it, thought it sounded like a little kid. But he let it go with Dickie.

Dickie held out his hand and pointed the remote at his black Lexus. The alarm made a quick and quiet beep. Dickie looked over the roof at Joe as he stepped toward the driver's side. "You hold on to the Mercedes. We'll square up later."

Dickie parked the Lexus in a handicap spot in front of the Black Bean Café, reached across Joe's legs for the glove box and grabbed the handicap sign he hung from the mirror.

Joe didn't ask what it was for, but as far as he could see, Dickie was healthy enough to walk a few spots to the front door.

They stepped out, and Dickie moved fast ahead of Joe toward the outside patio along the sidewalk. Even though he carried a little extra weight, most of it inside his round belly, he had plenty of pep in his step. Moved better than people half his age, said as soon as he got away from the cold winters up north it was like someone flicked a switch inside him.

They sat at a small cast-iron table with a red umbrella over it, not the most comfortable chairs but the weather was nice. Hot, a bit humid, but early enough to enjoy it.

Dickie pulled out a twenty and handed it to Joe,

then pointed with his chin toward the entrance. "I buy, you fly."

Joe grabbed the bill, stood up and waited for Dickie to tell him what he wanted.

"Get me one of those caramel lattes, tell them extra whip cream. They give you hardly any unless you ask." He waved his hand back at Joe. "Get whatever you want. They have those Danishes here; get 'em fresh from that bakery down the block."

Joe turned from Dickie and walked into the Black Bean Café. He ordered himself a large black coffee and an Apple Danish, then had to wait another five minutes for Dickie's caramel latte.

He walked outside, two paper plates balanced in one hand with his to-go cup, and Dickie's latte in the other. No lids on either, and some of the sticky caramel from the latte spilled on his hand.

Dickie grabbed the cup, licked the caramel and some of the cream off the top. "So, Joe, I've been thinking. Seems to me the pay over there at that so-called newspaper place isn't exactly padding your pockets. You said so, a little while ago. Am I right?"

Joe shrugged. "I still get a small pension from the *Post*, so between the two…"

"Yeah, but I'm sure you could use a little extra cash. No?"

Joe had a feeling there was something Dickie wanted but at first gave him the benefit of the doubt. They'd spent a lot of time together over the years, but more often than not, there was a reason whenever they'd get together. He sipped his coffee and looked over the cup at Dickie. "Who couldn't use a little extra cash?" He put his cup on the table and leaned back in his chair. "Although luckily it's just me. The only mouth to feed is my own. Outside of rent, I don't have much to worry about."

Dickie pulled his sunglasses off his face and placed them on the table. He wiped his chubby hand across his eyes a couple of times. "You ever take a vacation or anything, Joey?" He stared back at Joe.

"Who needs a vacation when we live here in the Sunshine State?" He looked past Dickie at the cars moving by on Biscayne Boulevard.

Dickie rolled his eyes. "Come on, Joey. I'm being serious here. How long's it been?"

"What, since I had a vacation?" He shrugged.

"Cause it cost an arm and a leg. Right? Without extra cash, a lot of people can't swing it."

Joe had no idea where Dickie was going with it. He turned and watched an attractive middle-aged woman, probably his age, help an old man from the passenger side of a car she'd parked on the street a few spaces from where Dickie had parked.

Dickie sipped his latte. "Would you be interested in doing a little something on the side?"

Joe stared back at him.

Dickie said, "You still have your marbles. And you look to keep in good shape."

Joe laughed. "Dickie, I'm not sure I want to hear

where you're going with this."

"I always used to tell you, you would've made a good detective. You always had the nose, able to find what you were after. And, at least most of the time, nobody got hurt."

"Most of the time." Joe huffed out a laugh.

Dickie looked around the patio, most of the other customers in their own worlds or on their phones. He pushed his cup aside and leaned on the table toward Joe. "I'd like you to help me find someone."

Joe stared back at him. "No, Dickie. I'm sorry, but I'm not—"

"Hear me out, will you?" He reached for Joe's hand and gave it a squeeze, looked back and forth one more time. "This guy owes me money. A *lot* of money."

"Like how much?"

Dickie paused before he answered. "How much doesn't matter. Not yet. But listen. All I need you to do is find the guy. I'll take care of the rest."

Joe held his gaze on Dickie. "Why *me*?"

"What am I supposed to do, call the cops?" He laughed and leaned back from the table. "Tell 'em I got a guy, got a gambling debt I need squared?"

Joe sipped his black coffee and then placed it on the table, looked out toward the street. "What about Will? I could talk to him. He's got his license. I could talk to him and—"

"If I wanted to talk to Will, I wouldn't be here talking to you. I mean, I know he's a friend of yours. But he's not as smart as you. He's a photographer. What kind of brains does that take?"

4

JOE WAITED DOWNSTAIRS on the couch in Dickie's house, had a drink in one hand and his other arm up on the pillow. He stared ahead at the eighty-inch TV on the wall and listened to the sports news on twenty-four seven in Dickie's house even when he wasn't home. Joe heard steps on the stairs and turned, saw Scarlett walk off the last step in tight shorts and a bikini top.

She had keys dangling from her hand, her purse over her shoulder, and stepped in front of Joe. "Dickie said you're keeping the Mercedes? I don't know why you'd want it. It's old, although I guess you did mention you like that sort of thing." She winked at him and looked around the room, then walked toward the French doors at the back. She pulled both doors open and stared out into the yard with the in-ground pool and cobblestone patio. She turned and looked at Joe. "When's Dickie going to be back?"

Joe shrugged. "Not sure, but I'm supposed to give you a ride back to the shop, pick up the other car."

"He say which one? Hope it runs better than the Mercedes."

"It seems to run pretty well, doesn't it?"

"The Mercedes?" She nodded. "It does. But, oh... I just couldn't get used to it. And it's not something a woman my age needs to be driving around."

Joe cracked a smile. "But for an old man like me..."

She looked him over. "Old man? Are you even forty?"

"Forty-one."

"That's nothing," she said, then turned to close the French doors.

"But, yeah," Joe said. "I do like old things. I don't know, maybe I'm wrong. But I felt like things were better back in the day."

"Back in the day?" she said with a quick laugh. "Now, that certainly makes you sound *old*. 'Back in the day.' I'm sure that's something my grandfather used to say." She walked into the kitchen.

Joe followed her, stopped and leaned on the island with his drink.

She turned to him. "I was pretty impressed with your record collection," she said. "I'd love to get a better look at it one of these days."

Joe gazed into his glass and pretended he didn't pick up on whatever it was she might've been hinting at. He looked at his watch. "We should get going."

She turned and opened the refrigerator, leaned way over and reached into the bottom drawer.

Joe tried not to look, but he couldn't help but notice the way her legs poured out from her tight shorts.

Scarlett looked back at Joe, and he turned away as she straightened up. "You want to take a drink for the ride?"

He held up his empty glass. "One's enough, for now."

She had a plastic bottle of water in her hand she'd pulled from the fridge. "You want a water?"

"Oh. No, thank you. I don't drink out of plastic bottles."

She had a look on her face, her eyes somewhat narrowed, and cracked the top on the bottle, took a sip and placed it down on the island in front of Joe. "You're just an all-around good guy, aren't you." It was more of a statement than a question.

They both stared at each other from opposite ends of the island.

Joe swallowed hard, then turned for the door. "We should go."

Joe pulled up to his office in the Mercedes, parked

in the space reserved for Ralph Connor, the owner of the newspaper he worked for. But Ralph was hardly ever there. The small local newspaper he owned had been bought out by an international media conglomerate looking to capitalize on the hyper-local news market. And after forty years as the publisher, Ralph was at the tail end of the transition period he'd agreed to as part of the deal.

Joe hadn't seen Ralph in a few weeks. He wasn't even the one signing the checks any longer, so it didn't matter much to Joe whether he saw him or not.

Joe didn't even have his own desk. Not that it mattered because he did most of his writing outside the office. Either at home or a coffee shop or somewhere he could sit outdoors if it wasn't too hot.

But once in a while he'd need a desk or a computer at the office. And he'd have to use Lauren Reedsy's space.

Lauren, divorced and in her upper-thirties, was the newspaper's so-called social media manager.

Joe and Lauren had always gotten along well, going back to when they worked together at the *Post*. But they never had much of a relationship outside of work.

Joe walked inside the office and snuck up behind Lauren, with her eyes on her computer screen. She had earbuds in her ears, and Joe could hear the music she was listening to. He put his hand on her shoulder and she jumped three feet in the air, startled as she swung around in her chair and looked up at him and pulled the earbuds from her ears. "Jesus, Joe. How many times do I have to tell you not to scare me like that?"

He smiled with a shrug. "Sorry."

She turned back to the mess all over her desk. "I thought you weren't coming in until tomorrow?"

"I'm just here to pick up my assignment," Joe said. "If you weren't busy, I was going to use the computer. But it's not a big deal. I'll go back to the apartment or over to the coffee shop."

She turned in her seat again and studied his face. "You okay?"

He paused. "Had a long night. But, yeah, I'm okay."

"You sure?" She backed away, then looked down at her desk. "Just let me clean up the mess. I can get out of here for a little while."

Joe waved his hand. "No, please. Sit down. It's not a big deal." He turned and looked toward what had always been Mr. Connor's desk behind the glass surrounding a small office. The whole place had that open-concept, like they thought they'd created in Silicon Valley, but newspapers had been doing it for a hundred years. Mr. Connor was the only one with his private space, but he could see everything everyone was doing. But the light behind the glass was off, his office dark.

Lauren shuffled papers around and put them into

a pile, then lifted them up against her chest. "Please, Joe. Have a seat. I'll find a place to finish up." She pulled the papers tight against her chest and leaned her head to look at her watch without dropping anything. "How much time do you need?"

He shook his head. "Lauren, really. I can—"

She turned and headed for the door. "Joe, it's all yours."

The other six people in the office were all quiet, didn't even look up, as though he wasn't even there. Each of them had earbuds in their ears.

"What are you working on?" Lauren said.

"Me? Oh… it's nothing."

She looked at him like she knew better. "Nothing?"

Joe hesitated. "Nothing I want to tell you about."

5

JOE PUT STEVIE Wonder on the stereo and poured himself a vodka and cranberry. He sat at his kitchen table and lifted the cover on his laptop. He glanced at the time in the corner of the screen. It was two minutes past midnight. He knew he needed sleep, but the last thing he wanted to do was wake up early to write an article he knew he wouldn't want to write anymore by morning.

His writing assignments were horrible, mostly local stuff he was sure nobody really cared about. It was a far cry from the days of investigative reporting, with a lot more at stake than just getting words on the page. In fact, it was an ideal job for a kid at the time who wanted to be a cop as much as he wanted to be a writer, and found his career to be the perfect option.

He stared at the empty screen, but a knock at the door got him up from his seat. He peered through the peephole and pulled open the door.

Scarlett didn't hesitate a single moment and walked into his apartment, slammed the door behind her, and jumped on him. She wrapped her arms around his neck and hung her legs on his hips. She attacked him with her lips and passionately kissed him until she dropped her legs and put her feet on the floor.

"Scarlett, what the hell are you—"

She pushed him into the room with the couch and the fireplace and the shelves full of records.

But Joe pushed her away and held down both of her arms. "Stop it! We can't do this…"

She stared into his eyes and ignored him. She looped her arms around his neck and led him backward to the couch, then let go and shoved him back with both hands.

His legs were weakened by his lack of sleep and the three or four vodka cranberries he'd already put back.

Scarlett jumped on top of him and kissed him.

"Higher Ground" came out of the speakers.

Joe used a little more force and pushed himself out from under her. She fell to the floor and landed on her back when he got up. He grabbed her hands and pulled her to her feet. "I'm sorry," he said. "I can't do this."

She had a pouty look on her face. "You don't want to?" She bit her lower lip and held it, her eyes on his. "I can't get you out of my mind."

He paused. "I can't."

She hadn't moved, stood in front of him with his back to the couch. She brushed her blonde hair from her face and tucked a strand over her ear, her eyes still on him. "I'm very disappointed. Especially after I already told you Dickie's very understanding when it comes to—"

"Again, I'm very sorry. But it's not going to happen." Joe ran his hand back through his thick dark hair.

She stepped closer to him and placed her hands on his chest. "You don't find me attractive?"

This time he pushed her aside and squeezed past her. He walked to the kitchen and picked his drink up off the table. He took a sip, then turned to her. "I have work I need to finish."

She looked toward his glass. "Aren't you going to ask if I want a drink?"

Joe didn't answer, then looked past her toward the sliding glass doors and the bright lights from the buildings across the street. "What are you doing over here this late, anyway?"

She shrugged. "Just thought I'd take a shot." She smiled, her gaze fixed on Joe.

He turned to the cabinet, took out a glass and fixed her a drink with ice and cranberry juice.

She took it from his hand and reached into the purse hung on her shoulder. She pulled out a joint and a lighter and held the joint between her two fingers, like a cigarette, and gave it a light. "You smoke?"

Joe stared at the tightly rolled joint. "It's been a while."

She took a hit and held it in, turned, and looked around his apartment, then blew out a stream of smoke. "I don't know if I told you this already, but I really like your apartment. It's different."

He took another sip from his glass but didn't respond to what she'd said. "So, you drove all the way over here for—"

"For you?" She shrugged. "I didn't think you'd mind. I thought we had a connection." She smiled, took another hit and blew it up toward the ceiling. She sipped her drink and spoke into the glass. "I guess I was mistaken?"

"No, that's not it. Come on now, Scarlett. It's just not my thing. Dickie's a friend of mine. I mean, I guess if that weren't the case, then maybe..." He didn't finish what he knew he couldn't say. He walked past her to his turntable. The music had stopped, and he flipped the album over. He turned the knob and lowered the volume. He didn't like silence at all and played music whenever he could. But when he was writing, the music had to be different. He listened to instrumental music, like classical or jazz.

Scarlett wet the ends of her fingers, pressed them together on the lit end of the joint to put it out. She placed it on the counter. "I won't tell Dickie a thing," she said. She took a step toward Joe. "He's home, sleeping like a baby. He took Benadryl before I left a few hours ago. He'll be knocked out till morning."

Joe shook his head. "Whether he'd know or not isn't the point. He's my friend."

Scarlett rolled her eyes. Her lids had closed a bit more from the pot, her eyes slightly red. "You really think he's your friend?" she said. "I mean, do you really consider him your friend? I mean, if you're such good friends, I mean, then how come you didn't know anything about me?"

Joe knew she was stoned. How many times had she said, "I mean?" He walked into the kitchen, leaned back against the counter and sipped his drink. "I've known him for a long time. We've helped each other out. More than once."

She followed Joe and stood in front of him, then tipped her head back and finished whatever was left of her drink. She held out the empty glass. "Can I have some water?"

Joe stepped around her and opened the refrigerator, pulled out a green glass bottle of sparkling water. He took the glass from Scarlett and filled it, handed it back to her and left the bottle out on the counter. He looked at his watch. "I'm sorry, but I really do have to get to work."

She sipped the water, then held it up toward the light. She looked into the glass and laughed. "Wow, that's super bubbly." She drank the rest, then put the glass on the table next to his laptop. "Sorry... I'm pretty stoned."

Joe watched her turn and walk toward his shelves full of records. He wondered what her deal was. He had to assume she wasn't as interested in Dickie as Dickie might've been led to believe. Joe figured their relationship had to have been about money.

He hoped, for Dickie's sake, he was wrong. He said, "What's the story with you and Dickie?"

But she didn't even try for a second to tell him anything other than what he'd already assumed. "He takes care of me. Buys me nice things."

"Do you love him?" The words came out and right away Joe wished they hadn't. It felt weird the way he said it.

She looked across the room at Joe but didn't answer.

Joe put his empty glass in the sink. He'd had enough for the night. "I'm just not comfortable with you being here. In fact, I'd prefer he didn't know you came by, if that's all right."

"I told you, he's out cold till morning. He won't even pee until I wake him up at seven."

Joe's eyes went to the joint Scarlett had left on the counter. He thought maybe it'd make the boring story he had to write a little more interesting. He'd written plenty of stories before while high, but it'd been a long time.

Scarlett walked over to the records, fingered through them like she had done the first night. She pulled out an album and held it up to him. "Can you play this?" She flipped it over and looked at the back. "I like the Rolling Stones."

Joe walked toward her and took the album from her hands. He removed the Stevie Wonder album from the turntable and swapped them out. And as soon as he turned to Scarlett, she grabbed him the way she had when she first walked in, her arms tight around the back of his neck.

She pulled him into her.

He didn't resist right away. With a few drinks in him, he was afraid he didn't have the willpower he needed.

They kissed, but it didn't last.

He pushed her back and slipped out from under her arms. "You're going to have to leave," he said. He reached for the knob on the stereo and turned off the music. "Please, go home to Dickie."

She had a look on her face, more annoyed than anything. She leaned over and picked her purse off the floor. She stared at Joe for a few seconds, then turned and walked for the door. She paused, pulled it open and walked out, slammed it closed behind her without another word.

6

JOE WOKE UP anxious, had no idea what he wrote but knew he got something done. He looked toward the other side of the bed, fairly certain he'd slept alone, but his head was not clear enough yet to be sure.

Once the cobwebs cleared, he was relieved nothing happened with Scarlett. As attractive as she was, he knew he did the right thing. And there was something about her he didn't like... something more than the fact she had no problem fooling around behind Dickie's back.

And Joe wasn't buying what she'd said, that Dickie'd be okay with it. He knew Dickie well enough to know there'd be no way he was.

He went into the bathroom and threw water on his face, wet his hair to keep it from sticking up, and brushed his teeth. He was already late for a meeting with his friend Will, although at least he'd missed the heavier traffic.

He picked up his phone plugged into the wall with the charger and saw he had a message from Lauren. She wanted him to call her back, so he shot her a text and said he'd call her later.

Joe took the stairs up to Will's office. And by the time he got to his floor, he was only five minutes late. Not too bad. He walked past the other offices, each one not much bigger than a walk-in closet, and wondered if that was something he could use. Give him a place to put his head down and get his work done without being distracted. If that were even possible.

The office building didn't seem to be that old but had a musty smell to go with the brown paneling on the walls.

Joe stopped in front of office suite number three-oh-seven, glanced at the sign that said Capello, Inc., and knocked on the door.

"It's open," said a voice from the other side.

Joe turned the knob and walked in to the smell of cigarette smoke. He faced Will Capello seated behind the desk in the flowered Hawaiian shirt he wore a lot. "I thought you quit smoking?"

Will gave Joe a nod from behind the desk. "I did. A few times." He reached across the desk and shook Joe's hand. "You look good," he said, and gestured for Joe to sit in the chair across from him.

"You look good yourself," Joe said, although he wasn't sure he was telling the truth.

Will pushed aside some papers on his desk and slid them into a single pile. "You want a coffee?"

Joe shook his head and looked at the stack of newspapers on top of the bookcase. Will had a camera tripod on the floor behind him with a camera attached to it. "How's business?"

Will followed Joe's eyes to the camera and shifted in his seat. "Not the most interesting photography subjects, but I've got some work with a local insurance company. Small-time fraud cases, mostly. Not exactly what I thought I'd be doing at this point, but…"

"Puts food on the table, right?"

Will leaned back in his chair. He pulled his shirt over his fat belly pouring over his belt. "As you can see, I eat plenty."

Joe looked away, his eyes on the camera again. "Is that what you've been up to? Insurance fraud investigations?"

Will shrugged. "If you want to call it that. I follow a guy around, shoot some pictures and call it a day. It's easy money, to be honest."

"You did get your license though?"

"My private investigator's license?" He nodded. "I had to. My contact at the insurance company said there was too much liability for them without it." He shrugged. "I'm not sure they were bullshitting me or not, but…" He turned and looked toward the window. "I've had a couple of random clients land in my lap. One of 'em's been repeat business, woman with a husband doesn't seem to care he gets caught. But she pays me to follow him… usually see him with a different broad each time. Then the wife, she stays with him anyway."

"Sounds like you're keeping busy?"

"Yeah, I guess so." Will folded his hands together on the desk and leaned forward. "So rather than beat around the bush… you mentioned in your message you might need my help?"

"Catching up with an old friend is beating around the bush?" He turned and looked behind him through the open door and into the hallway.

Will got up and walked around the desk. "You need me to close that?" He didn't wait for Joe to answer and closed it anyway, then sat behind his desk.

Joe said, "I had coffee with Dickie Caldwell."

Will shifted his eyes toward the floor, then looked back at Joe. "Dickie Caldwell, huh?"

Joe leaned forward in the chair, his elbows on his knees. "He asked me to help him find someone."

Dickie raised his eyebrows. "You?" He snorted out a laugh and shook his head. "I told you this would happen, didn't I? All those years you got information out of crooks like him, only a matter of time you'd need to pay back the favor."

"That's not it at all," Joe said. "Far as I'm concerned, Dickie and I've been square for quite some time. But he's not asking me to do it for free. He's going to pay me. A pretty good chunk of change, too."

Will leaned forward on the desk, a little more interested. "Who're you looking for?"

"Well, the thing is, as far as Dickie knows, the man's name is Matthew Doyle. But he's not sure it's even his real name."

"Who is he? A customer?"

Joe nodded. "Stiffed him for ninety grand."

Will's lower lip stuck out. "That's a good amount of money." He squinted his eyes. "Don't take this the wrong way, Joe... but why's he asking you to do it?" He shrugged. "I mean, it's not really your thing. You should've told him to call me." He turned and looked at his private investigator's license hung with the corners curled on the wall, a single thumbtack holding it up. "Sounds like he needs a private investigator. Not a—"

"I'd like you to help me find him," Joe said. "I'll split the fee with you... whatever Dickie's going to pay me."

"I thought you said he was paying you a chunk of change."

"He is. But I didn't give him my word I'd do it yet. We still need to discuss the details."

"You tell him you were going to ask me to help you?"

Joe looked at the floor before he lifted his gaze back to Will. "I think it's just best we keep it between us for now. Dickie wants to keep things quiet. If he thinks I mentioned it to someone else…"

Will rolled his eyes. "Oh, I get it. He doesn't think the guy with the camera's worth a shit. You were the one got all the credit… being a man of words. The photographer was just your sidekick. Is that what he thinks?"

"I'm not sure that's the case at all. But you know how it is. Dickie and I are friends. He trusts me. And I don't think he trusts a lot of people."

"I did a lot for the son of a bitch myself. How quickly he forgets."

Joe cleared his throat. "Are you done? Why does it matter? I told you I'd split it with you. Fifty-fifty. Down the middle. All you have to do is keep it quiet, so Dickie doesn't find out."

"And, what, you get all the credit?"

Joe took a breath and leaned his head back, looked up at the ceiling. "Christ, Will. Why do you have to make a big deal out of the smallest things?"

Will slid his hand between the buttons on his shirt and scratched his chest. "It'll just be me and you?"

Joe cracked a smile. "Like old times. And I'm meeting with Lauren, see if she'd be willing to help us out, too. But don't worry, I'll pay her for her time out of my share."

"What do you have so far?" Will said.

Joe pulled out his phone and remembered he was

supposed to call Lauren back. "Nothing yet. But as soon as I talk to Lauren…"

7

THE DOORBELL RANG inside Dickie's house. Joe turned with his back to the door. He looked out around the courtyard and at his car, the yellow Mercedes, parked in the circular driveway.

He turned when the door opened. Scarlett was on the other side.

"Oh, it's you," she said. Cold as ice. She left the door open and walked back inside without another word to Joe. He watched her from the top step until she turned and looked back at him over her shoulder. "Aren't you going to come inside?"

Joe was somewhat surprised by the way she acted, clearly insulted he'd pushed her away the night before. He followed her in and stopped just inside the door.

Scarlett sat on the white couch in front of the TV and put her feet up. She picked up an *Entertainment Weekly* magazine and acted as if Joe wasn't even there. She flipped a page without looking up and said, "Dickie'll be right down."

A moment later, Dickie rounded the corner in a silk-like black shirt buttoned down, the hem hung out over his shorts. He had a Manila folder in his hand and brown leather sandals on his feet. "Scar, hon, you make any coffee?"

Scarlett looked at him from over the top of her magazine, then tossed it on the glass coffee table in front of her. She got up and glanced at Joe out of the corner of her eye, stepped in front of Dickie and gave him a kiss. "I'll make a fresh pot for you and your friend."

Your *friend*? Joe wondered what that was all about but let it go, wasn't about to go into any of it with Dickie. He looked at the yellow paint on her toenails but tried not to watch her walk toward the kitchen. He glanced at Dickie. And as he suspected, Dickie was looking at him.

"Come on," Dickie said. "We'll go sit out back." He stepped outside through the French doors behind the couch and walked toward the pool. But he stopped and turned to the open doors and yelled in for Scarlett. "Scar, bring us two cups outside when it's ready." He continued toward the table by the pool.

Joe wondered what Scarlett had told Dickie about the night before. He was afraid to ask. He, of course, hoped she hadn't said a word, but had a feeling keeping her mouth shut wasn't her thing. But he wanted to keep the story straight in case Dickie asked any questions, although it didn't matter much if their stories didn't match up. Dickie knew him well enough he'd trust his word. At least he hoped that would be the case.

Dickie sat at the table under the pergola with a couple of fans running overhead. He watched Joe settle into his seat. "So, how's the car?" he said.

"It's a lot different than driving the Taurus."

Dickie let out a laugh. "Well, it's not a Ford, Joe. I can tell you that much."

Joe looked off past the pool at the small pond with the fountain in the center. He liked the bubbling sound coming from it and thought how he wouldn't mind having a yard like this to write in.

"You like driving it?" Dickie said, clearly not satisfied with Joe's answer.

"Yes, I like it."

Dickie pushed the folder he had in his hand, across the table. "This is all I've got. Hopefully it'll get you started. Like I said, it might not be his real name. Maybe it is. But those pictures'll hopefully get you headed in the right direction."

Joe opened the folder and looked at the photos. "This is Matt Doyle?"

Dickie turned and looked back at the house. "Do me a favor... like I said, do all you can to keep it quiet. And I don't want Scarlett knowing anything about it either. She doesn't need to know everything about me, all right?" He stared back at Joe.

"Yeah, no problem at all." He had already told Will to keep things between them and had no reason to tell Dickie that Will was going to help him. He looked at the photo in his hand. "He lives in Miami?"

"Yeah, but not at the address I had for him. Turns out he was never there. People had never even heard of him."

"So you've already tried to find him?"

"Not me, personally. I sent a couple of guys over. But these two knuckleheads... they've got the muscle but"—he tapped on the side of his head and nodded his chin toward Joe—"not even a quarter the brains you have. They wouldn't find a piece of shit under their own pillows."

Joe kept his eyes on the photos, looked at the two and tried to place the face. He thought he looked familiar but had the characteristics a lot of guys do in Miami: hair slicked back, gold chain around his neck. Joe swore he could smell the guy's cologne just looking at the photo.

One of the doors opened from the patio and Scarlett walked out with a cup of coffee in each hand.

Joe closed the folder and leaned his arms on it as if he could hide it from view.

Scarlett glanced at it and placed a cup in front of Joe, the other in front of Dickie.

He put his hand on her ass and winked at her. "Thank you, beautiful." He pointed to her and looked at Joe as she walked away without a word. "She's something else, isn't she?"

Joe watched her walk through the door.

She glanced back at him, then cracked a smile and closed the door. He pushed the coffee aside and opened the folder again, pulled out a piece of paper. "This is what he owes you?"

Dickie said, "I told you, ninety grand. Son of a bitch paid me on time the first few times, so I opened up the purse for him a bit more. Next thing you know, he stops taking my calls." He pointed toward the folder. "The address I had is on there, but like I said, he's not there."

"What makes you think it's not his real name?"

"I don't know one way or the other. I'm just speculating. Guys do it sometimes to protect themselves. I was a fool for believing the guy wasn't full of shit. I can usually tell right away." He nodded toward the folder. "There's a business card in there. Some kind of independent dealer for a security company."

"Security?" Joe looked for the card inside the folder.

"Oh, I don't know. Alarms. House alarms, you know? Stuff like that. But I called the number on that card, and it went to some other business that sells pool filters or something like that."

"Nobody knew anything about him?" Joe found the card between a few loose pieces of paper. He held it up. "Viper Security Systems." He flipped it over and looked at the back. "That sounds familiar."

Dickie shrugged. "Like I said, you find the guy… that's all I need you to do. But just in case you have anything you're worried about, he's smaller than you. Maybe the same height, but he doesn't have your build. You won't have anything to worry about if by chance you run into any trouble." Dickie cracked a slight smile. "Guy like you doesn't have to be concerned, got enough muscle on you, built like a brick shithouse. Especially for a writer."

"So how much are we talking here?"

Dickie gazed across the table at Joe. "I don't care about the money. It's the principle. You find him, let me know where he is, you take half. Forty-five grand."

"Forty-five grand?" Joe was shocked. But he liked it. "Shit. Thanks, Dickie."

"Don't thank me yet. You'll have to find the bastard." He looked back toward the house, then leaned on the table. "In fact, you deliver him to me. And if I don't need to involve the two knuckleheads, I'll get you another ten grand on top of it."

8

JOE SAT ALONE at Hal's Eastside Diner and looked out the window from the last table on the far left. He watched Lauren walk across the lot from her car.

She was late. She always was.

She walked inside and looked left to right. She didn't see Joe in the booth until he put up his hand and waved to her. She gave him a nod and hurried past the other tables, threw her oversized purse into the booth and plopped down across from him. "Sorry I'm late." She brushed her hair from her face. "Traffic's a bitch."

Joe looked at the purse. "You traveling?"

She gave him a funny look and shook her head. "Traveling?"

He smiled and glanced toward the bag. "What's in there?"

She shrugged. "I don't know. Just my stuff." She

caught the waitress's eye and smiled with an excited wave. "Hi, Jennie!"

Jennie was an older woman who'd been at Hal's long before she got old. Joe remembered her when he was a kid. She stopped at their table and pulled her pad from the pocket in her smock. She took the pen out from behind her ear and smiled at Lauren. "You know what you want? Or you want me to come back?" She winked at Joe. "You must be starving, sitting here alone all morning."

Lauren again pushed her hair from her face. "I'm sorry, I'm not one for being on time."

Joe pushed his cup closer to Jennie. "I'll have a little more of that delicious diner coffee while we wait for Lauren to settle in."

Lauren opened the menu and closed it without even looking. "I'll have a grilled cheese. And a soup of the day... whatever it is."

Jennie poured more coffee into Joe's cup and took the menu from Lauren. "It's chicken noodle."

Lauren looked at an older gentleman at the counter, sipping his soup. "You have tomato?"

"Soup?" Jennie nodded and wrote in her pad. "Grilled cheese with tomato soup?"

Joe ordered a turkey club, and Jennie turned and walked into the kitchen.

Lauren pulled a notebook from her bag and put it up on the table, grabbed a pen and had it ready to write. She glanced up at Joe. "I'd love to think you called me to have lunch without needing something.

But I know better."

Joe was caught off guard. "What? Why, I, we've gone out before without, I mean." He shrugged. "I'm sorry. It's just that I—"

He stopped when Jennie stopped and put a mug of tea in front of Lauren. She topped off Joe's cup with more coffee.

He took a sip and made a face. "I wish they had better coffee."

"You just told her it was delicious."

"I was being polite. Although… it *is* my third cup."

They both sat quiet until Lauren looked up at him. "I'm sorry, Joe. I didn't mean to make you uncomfortable like that. But, I don't know, I was just thinking on the ride over here about how we've worked together for quite a few years. And we've never once gone anywhere that didn't have something to do with work or some assignment you needed my help with."

"Are you sure about that?" Joe said.

Lauren gave him a funny look and sipped her tea, keeping her eyes on him over the rim.

"Okay, well, don't forget you were married for a lot of those years. And you said it yourself: Mister Antisocial never wanted to leave the house." Joe sipped his coffee, then leaned back in the booth with his arm up along the back.

Lauren was younger than Joe but only by a handful of years. Sometimes she looked and acted older than she actually was. Maybe it was that she didn't always wear makeup, or that she often had a frazzled look about her. Even the clothes she wore sometimes made her look a bit frumpy. Not to mention the way the glasses she wore magnified her eyes.

But Joe always liked her. They had something between them, but he could never put his finger on what it was. Not that he ever thought about it much or wondered if there was anything to it, other than she was just a person he enjoyed being around. And he knew she always worried about him.

Lauren leaned with her breasts rested on top of her hands folded on the table. "So why don't you tell me what this is all about? Before Jennie brings us our food?"

Joe let out a slight laugh and wished for a moment he could've told her it was nothing, that he just wanted to have lunch with her. But she'd see right through it. And Joe was never one to lie.

"I ran into Dickie Caldwell. Actually, I was at his shop to get some work done." He looked out the window toward the Mercedes. "Although... I ended up junking the Taurus. Dickie gave me a Mercedes to drive for now."

Lauren turned and looked outside. "The yellow one?"

Joe nodded. "Like they say, I drove the Taurus into the ground. But I kept my foot on the gas."

She smiled. "It fits you."

"The Mercedes?"

"Yeah. If it was a new one that cost a lot of money, I couldn't see you driving it. But... it's definitely a Joe Sheldon kind of car." She laughed and sipped her tea. "I swear you were born in the wrong era, like you traveled in time from the middle of the century."

Joe shrugged. "You never know."

Lauren pushed her cup aside. "So, how's Dickie?"

"Well, he's got a girlfriend. She lives with him. And she's half his age."

"Good for him, right?"

"I don't know. There's something off with her. I'm just afraid she's after something more than his good looks."

Lauren shrugged and straightened out from the table. "What makes you..."

Before she could finish, the waitress dropped off their plates and put two iced waters on the table. "Anything else?"

Joe and Lauren both shook their heads and the waitress walked away.

Lauren stirred her soup. "Dickie's a big boy," she said. "And I'm sure he knows to keep his hand over his wallet, if that's what you mean."

Joe poured a glob of ketchup on his plate, dipped a fry in it and stuck it in his mouth. He finished what was in his mouth and said, "You date a woman half your age, and—"

"Does this have something to do with why you

wanted to meet?"

He took a bite of his sandwich, then wiped his mouth with the paper napkin. "I'm doing some work for Dickie. A side job."

"Doing what?" She sipped her soup and looked up at him from over the spoon.

"Well, it's just a way to make some extra money." Joe wiped both hands and slid the napkin under his plate. He leaned back in the booth. "He wants me to help him find someone."

Lauren gave a slight tilt to her head. "He wants you to find someone? You sure that's a good idea, Joe?"

"I could use the money. And all I have to do is find the guy. Nothing else to it."

Lauren dipped her grilled cheese in her soup and took a bite. "Is it someone who owes him money?"

Joe looked around the diner. "Guy owes him ninety grand."

Lauren's eyes opened wide behind her glasses. "That's a lot. At least it is to *me*."

"You're not kidding it's a lot. The guy got in over his head, then disappeared. Dickie claimed he opened up his purse for him; next thing he knows, he stops taking his calls. The guy's phone was disconnected. Dickie even had one of his lackeys go by where the guy works. Apparently nobody's ever heard of him." Joe reached into his pocket and tossed the business card on the table. "Dickie's not sure it's even his real name."

Lauren picked it up. "Matt Doyle? But he made up the name?"

Joe said, "Went through a lot of trouble. Dickie got careless. For whatever reason, he trusted the guy."

Lauren looked at both sides of the business card and placed it in front of Joe. "I assume this is why you've invited me to lunch?" She took another bite of her grilled cheese. She placed it down, wiped each finger with the napkin, then folded it a few times, and stuck it under her plate.

"Will's going to help. He was reluctant initially, offended Dickie didn't call him first."

"But you were always Dickie's boy."

Joe picked up the glass of water and took a sip. "Will's got his private investigator's license."

Lauren looked surprised. "I thought he was into bail bonds?"

"He was." Joe grabbed the tab and placed a couple of bills on top of it, slid it toward the edge of the table. "So, can you help?"

"Have I ever said *no* to you?" she said.

9

JOE WAS OUT at Bayfront Park with a notebook, trying to write, when his phone rang. He'd normally turn it off when he wrote but knew Lauren would be calling.

"Hey," he said when he answered. "Don't tell me you already found something?"

She laughed. "I wish it'd be that easy. But I did find three Matt Doyles living in Florida. One is here in Miami, but he's only twenty-three."

"This guy's supposedly closer to forty. Late thirties, according to Dickie."

She said, "But Dickie's not even sure it's his real name, right?"

Joe stood up from the bench and started back for the car. "It's just what we have to work with."

"Okay, so I'd already eliminated the kid. So out of the other two, only one has relatives in Miami. I compiled as many photos as I could online, mostly social media posts. Maybe we could show Dickie, see if any of them match up. There's one picture I can link back to a profile for a Matthew Doyle, but it's of a woman. That doesn't make much sense. Looks more like she didn't even know her picture was being taken."

"There's no name?"

"For who, the woman? No, I told you, it's a profile photo for a Matthew Doyle. Unless…"

Lauren didn't finish.

"Unless what?" Joe said.

"Nothing. Listen, I have a couple of addresses for people I believe to be related to this guy."

"So, you're working with the assumption Matt Doyle's his real name?"

"Yeah, like we talked about."

"And we'll work back from there. If this guy isn't who we're looking for, then I'm not sure how we'd find someone we have no photo of and don't know his real name."

"If that's the case, Joe, then I don't even know where you'd begin."

"Let's not worry about it now. Can you email me those names and addresses?"

"I already did."

Joe smiled into the phone. "You're wonderful, Lauren. I don't think I tell you that enough."

"I don't think you *ever* told me that."

The phone was quiet on both ends.

"What else do you want me to do?" Lauren said.

"Just sit tight for now. I'll let you know what I find."

"You don't want me to come with you?" she said.

Joe thought about it before he answered. "I can't say for sure it'd be safe."

"You don't think I can handle it?"

"It's not that you can't handle it, it's just that…"

"You like to work alone. I know. I get it. Joe Sheldon, the Lone Ranger."

"That's not true. Why would I have called you and Will if I wanted to do this alone."

They were both quiet.

Joe said, "How about I just go find the guy, wrap this up, then you and I go out for dinner to celebrate?"

"Dinner? For what, another grilled cheese at Hal's?"

He laughed. "No. I mean a real dinner. Somewhere nice."

She didn't answer right away.

"Do we really have to wait to find the guy? Because, if you don't, I'm going to be sitting around waiting."

"Oh, uh…"

"I'm just saying, do you have to wrap it up like it's my reward for helping you? Can't we just go out, have a nice dinner together? For fun? I don't have to tell you that I haven't been out much at all since the divorce. It would be nice."

"Yes. Of course. Why not, right?"

Lauren sighed into the phone. "Do you have to make it sound like you're doing me a favor?"

He didn't think that's how it came across. At least he didn't intend for it to sound that way.

"We've always had fun together," she said. "At least on the job. And really, Joe, I'm not trying to put you on the spot. If you don't want to, it's all right."

"What? No, come on. You're not putting me on the spot. Not at all. I told you I wanted to take you out, didn't I? Let's do it. How about tonight?"

"I can't do it tonight. But what about tomorrow? Unless you have plans?"

Joe nodded into the phone. "Perfect. I'll pick you up in the Mercedes."

Lauren paused. "I think I'll just meet you there. I'll take a cab. That way you're not obligated to take me home. If it all goes well, you can give me a ride back home."

"So it's a date?" he said.

"I don't know if you need to call it that"—she let out a slight laugh—"but let's plan on it. Tomorrow night. Just let me know the place."

Joe was at his kitchen table and opened the email Lauren had sent him. He printed the names and addresses of anyone in the area related to Matt Doyle. Whether or not this was the Matt Doyle he was looking for remained to be seen.

He picked up his phone and called Lauren. "Hey," he said, "aren't there any photos with these names?"

"I thought I told you I couldn't find any. I found it a little strange myself, but you never know why. Some people steer clear of having their identities online. It's not that hard. And one of the names is an older woman in her seventies."

"I get that. The only photo you'll find of me is an old one from the *Post*. I think I was twenty-four when it was taken."

"Well, you're not quite seventy; you're just not very social online. Most people have just given up and put themselves out there. Or someone else does without them knowing."

"I know. What a world."

10

JOE TOOK THE elevator to the twelfth floor of the luxury apartments on Southeast Third Avenue. An old woman passed him and stepped into the elevator before he even stepped out. When Joe turned back to look at her, the doors had already closed. He walked down the hall and turned the corner, stopped in front of Apartment nine-oh-six. He rang the bell and waited no more than three seconds. A man Joe assumed was Daniel Doyle opened the door and looked out at Joe.

"Are you Daniel?" Joe said.

"Who are you?" the man said.

"I'm sorry to bother you, but I'm looking for your cousin, Matthew Doyle."

The man looked at Joe. "Are you a cop?"

"No. Do you know where he is?"

"Does he owe you money?"

"I'm just trying to find him, that's all I can tell

you."

The man shrugged. "I haven't seen him. But if you do find him, tell him to bring back my wife's diamond ring." He started to close the door, and Joe put his hand out to stop it.

"He took your wife's diamond ring?"

"I'm sure he did. All I know is I opened up my home to him and her ring disappeared."

Joe looked along the hall. "He just took it? It wasn't on her finger?"

The man paused before he answered. "My wife was stung by a bee. Matt was here with his girlfriend, who helped her. Or so we thought. She helped remove the ring from my wife's swollen finger. And after they left, we realized the ring was missing. I called him and he didn't answer. I'm not even sure he has the same phone anymore."

"That's what I've heard," I said. "Is he still with the girlfriend?"

Daniel shrugged. "Like I said, I haven't seen or heard from him."

"How well do you know *her*?" Joe said.

"The girlfriend? Hardly at all. They stayed here for a couple nights; that was it. Didn't even tell us they were leaving, took off after the bee sting incident."

"Name?"

"Oh, uh, her name was Pam. At least that's what he called her. But I'm pretty perceptive. I was suspicious of her from the moment they showed up at my door. He'd say her name, and unless she's got a hearing problem, half the time she wouldn't even look until he said it two or three times."

Joe took his hand off the door. Daniel didn't seem as anxious to slam it in his face.

"Didn't you call the cops?" Joe said.

"About the ring?" He shook his head. "I guess I hoped I was wrong. But the more time passed, I'm sure they took it."

"But why didn't you call the cops?"

"I don't know. It's just that... I didn't."

Joe wondered what the guy wanted to say.

Daniel said, "So, are you some kind of private detective or something? You're a big guy, but you don't look like a hit man."

Joe looked himself over. "No, I'm neither." He turned and looked over his shoulder. "Well, thank you for your time." He started down the hall and didn't look back. He didn't hear the door close but stepped onto the elevator as soon as the doors opened.

Lauren had called Joe with another name she thought he should check out. The woman's name was Morgan, but she was still working on a last name. Lauren only said she connected the dots to this woman but didn't explain much else. Joe didn't care to hear it either as long as he had another lead he could follow up with.

Joe knocked, and when the door opened it took him a moment to get the words out of his mouth. She was movie-star beautiful, a lot of hair but not puffy, like some of the women around Miami. Straight and blonde, not even a hint of darkness at the roots.

He never could help but pay attention to minor details.

"Are you Morgan?"

She smiled back at him with her big bright eyes.

"My name's Joe Sheldon. Someone told me you might be able to help me find a man named Matt Doyle."

She shook her head. "I don't mind at all. Not one bit…" She backed up from the door, not concerned in the least about letting a stranger into her home.

Joe walked in and smelled the pot odor mixed with the sweetness of women's perfume. "So how do you know Matt?" he said as soon as she closed the door.

She gestured toward the couch. "Have a seat if you'd like." She stepped from the room toward the kitchen. "Can I get you a drink?"

"No, not right now. Thanks."

She came out with a highball in her hand, took a sip and sat in a chair across from Joe. "Matt was my boyfriend, if you want to call him that, for about a week. But then he met my sister."

"He dates your sister? Is her name Pam, by any chance?"

"Pam?" She let out a slight laugh. "No." She followed Joe's eyes to the unlit joint in the ashtray in front of him. "You can light that if you'd like some. It's pretty good stuff."

He hesitated to answer, thought about it until she got up and grabbed it herself, pulled a lighter from her pocket and lit the end. She took a hit and handed it over to him. Holding her breath, she said, "Here."

Joe swallowed, then grabbed it from her. "Maybe one hit." He put it up to his lips and inhaled but didn't hold it in for more than a handful of seconds.

"What is it you want with Matt?"

Joe got up from the couch and handed her the joint. "He has something that belongs to a friend of mine. I'm just trying to locate him, see if he'd be willing to talk."

"Is it money?" Morgan said.

Joe nodded. "Something like that."

"He owes a lot of people money. So tell your friend to get in line." She smiled, took another hit and handed it back to Joe.

Joe reached for the joint and took another hit. This time he held it in his lungs for a little longer. He exhaled and said, "Any chance he owes you?"

"Matt?" She shook her head. "I'm not dumb enough to give him a thing."

Joe thought for a moment, then realized he still had the joint in his hand. He handed it back to Morgan but she shook her head and nodded toward the ashtray. "Just leave it in there."

Joe did as she said and walked to the window. He looked out toward the parking lot below. "When was the last time you saw him?"

"I'd say a month or two. Maybe more. I haven't really thought about it much."

"What about your sister?"

"What about her?"

"She still with him?"

Morgan got up from her chair and went in the kitchen without an answer but came back out with two tall glasses of water. She handed one to Joe. "I don't know if she's still with him. I hope not."

"You don't know?"

She shrugged and sat back in the chair. "Those two have been on and off for as long as they've been together. She spent some time in jail, and I thought she learned her lesson."

"What'd she do?"

"She had a job in a nursing home, stole some jewelry from a woman. Did six months at the women's Reception Center in Ocala." She sipped her water. "I haven't seen her since before she went in."

"No?"

"Sometimes you think she's got a good head on her shoulders, other times…" She sighed and shrugged one shoulder. "Never was a good judge of men."

Joe had already started to feel the pot go to his

head and regretted doing it in the first place. Maybe if it'd been under different circumstances…

"You know where I can find her?" he said.

Morgan let out a slight laugh and crossed one leg over the other, rested the glass on top of her thigh. "She's still my sister, you know. I don't think it'd make much sense for me to send some strange man after her."

"I told you, I just want to find Matt Doyle. I have no interest in bothering your sister."

"I'm not sure I want to be the one responsible for whatever it is you're going to do to Matt."

Joe shook his head. "I'm not going to do anything to him. I just need to know where he is."

She shook her head. "I'm sorry. I think I've said enough."

"I guess I understand." He got up from the couch and walked across the room toward the door. He stopped at the credenza to the right of the door and looked at the framed photos on top. He noticed Morgan in one of them, seated next to a woman younger but as beautiful as she was. He looked closer and his eyes almost popped out of his head. He pointed and turned to Morgan.

She was up from her chair and walking toward him. "Yeah, that's her."

"Your sister?" He looked back at the photo before he said another word. He was stoned and started to wonder if his mind was playing games. "That's your sister?" He looked one more time.

"Scarlett is your sister?"

11

JOE SAT WITH Dickie outside on the deck at Mickey Cho's Water Club, in the downstairs of the Hilton Hotel off Bayshore Drive.

Dickie liked it mostly for the sushi but said it had the best view of Biscayne Bay. Better than anywhere else in the area.

Joe was hesitant to tell Dickie about Scarlett's sister and thought maybe he'd be better off getting a feel for what Dickie knew about Scarlett and Matt Doyle. He assumed he knew nothing at all. Joe sipped his drink. "Does Scarlett know what you do? Or I should ask, does she know what I'm doing for you?"

Dickie used his chopsticks to pick up a piece of his tuna roll but dropped it in the soy he'd mixed with wasabi. He picked it up with his fingers and shoved the whole piece in his mouth. He held up his finger to Joe and wiped his mouth. "Well, you already know she does the books for me at the shop. So, she knows the place makes money. But I think she's smart enough to know I've got some other businesses."

"Is that a no?"

He shrugged. "I don't give her the details, if that's what you're asking." He used the chopsticks and again tried to pick up another piece of sushi; this time it made it up to his mouth. He ate it whole, grabbed the napkin and wiped his hands. "She doesn't ask a lot of questions. And I don't feel there's any reason she needs to know about our little arrangement. That's why I'd asked you to keep it between us."

Joe leaned back in his chair and looked out toward the bay. "You ever met any of her family?"

Dickie laughed. "I'm not sure she's in a hurry to bring a man my age home to mommy and daddy." He reached for another piece of sushi, but it slipped back down to the plate. He threw the chopsticks on the table and grabbed the tuna with his fingers, shoved the whole piece in his mouth. He sipped his drink, held up the chopsticks and looked them over. "I don't know why we even bother with these goddamn things. You go back a few thousand years before whoever it was invented chopsticks, you'll find they weren't really much of an improvement over what they used before."

"What they used *before*?"

Dickie nodded. "Yeah, fingers. You think eating

with two sticks makes more sense than using your own hands? Not me. I mean, a fork's a different story, but…" Dickie used his fingers and took the last piece of sushi from the first roll. He slipped it in his mouth and chewed, wiped his mouth and glanced across the table at Joe. "What makes you ask about Scarlett?"

Joe took a moment but decided not to answer Dickie. Pretend like he didn't hear him. "Do you know if she has any brothers or sisters in the area?"

"She's got a sister. But as far as I know they don't talk. At least not that I'm aware of. Guess they had a falling out of some sort."

"Morgan?"

Dickie had his glass up to his lips but stopped before he took a sip. He gave Joe a funny look. "How'd you know that?"

"I came across her name. Doing some research."

Dickie scratched the top of his balding head. "Research?" His face lost the pleasantness he normally tried to carry around. Got real serious. "I didn't ask you to research my…" He stopped. "Okay, Joe. You going to tell me what the hell you're getting at? You know me well enough to know I don't like beating around the bush." He pointed his stubby finger at Joe. "How do they say it in your business? Don't bury the lede?"

"That's not at all what that means, but…"

"Okay, well, whatever the hell it is, I know what you're doing. You're trying to hook me into something here. I know your tricks, Sheldon."

"I just came across her name, Dickie. That's the truth. I mean, how many women you know her age named Scarlett. And with a sister named Morgan?"

Dickie shrugged, loosened up a bit and cracked a smile. "Scarlett talked about her once or twice. One time when I asked her why her parents named her Scarlett, she said her father named her after Scarlett O'Hara. Mother wanted to name her Vivien, after Vivien Leigh. The actress who played her."

Joe nodded. "I know who she is." He picked up his glass, but it was empty other than an ice cube or two. "They still around?"

"Who?"

"The parents?"

"I don't think so." Dickie pushed the plate toward Joe. "What's the matter, you don't want to eat?"

"I'm not big on raw fish."

Dickie pulled the plate back, tried the chopsticks one more time and held on to the piece from the roll and shoved it in his mouth.

It was a little after five o'clock, and Joe stood in front of his bathroom sink. He wiped the fog from the mirror with the end of the towel hung over his shoulder, then foamed up his face. He hadn't shaved in a handful of days so pulled a brand-new razor from the package.

He slid the blade along his cheek two or three

times.

There was a knock at his door.

"Shit," he said. He wiped his hands with the towel and walked down the hall toward the front door. He stepped across the kitchen and looked through the peephole. He didn't see anybody outside and thought maybe he was hearing things. Or maybe it was one of the neighbors.

He turned and started back toward the bathroom but there was another knock. This time he didn't bother to look through the peephole. He just opened the door.

His hand was still on the knob when a man wearing a ski mask over his face crashed into Joe and slammed him to the floor. The man lifted his fist to strike Joe's face. But Joe hadn't wiped the shaving cream from his cheeks, and he turned his face just enough so the man's fist slid off without much impact and hit the floor.

Joe reached back for the towel that fell off his shoulder and wrapped it around the guy's neck. He twisted it into a knot and yanked the man down to the floor next to him. He flipped himself and was up on top. He straddled the guy and raised his hand to throw a punch. But he caught a glimpse of a shadow coming from the doorway.

Another man—this one short and stocky—had come into Joe's apartment. He tried to grab Joe's arm and get him off of his friend. But Joe threw an elbow back as the man reached for him from behind, caught the guy in the face, and knocked him back toward the open door.

The man under Joe worked his way out from under him. He tried to grab hold of Joe, but Joe was up on his feet and threw a punch. He felt a crack when he made contact with the man's jaw.

But the other one was up from the doorway. Joe caught a glimpse of him but it was too late. The man swung his arm with something cold and hard in his hand.

Joe almost fell backward and stumbled into the kitchen from the initial blow. He grabbed on to the edge of the counter to keep himself from falling. He put his hand to the back of his head and felt the warmth of his own blood run down the back of his neck and through his fingers. He was dazed. And before he could focus, he felt another crack. He dropped to his knees and closed his eyes, felt his face hit the floor, and everything went dark.

12

JOE HAD A bag of frozen peas up against the back of his head and tried to clean up most of the mess in his apartment. He thought about calling the cops but knew getting them involved would open up a whole can of worms he didn't think should be open.

With one free hand, he cleaned up the place, picked up his albums the two goons had thrown on the floor, although luckily none of his favorites. They smashed dishes, tipped over chairs, and pulled drawers from the cabinets and left them on the floor.

But as far as he could tell, nothing had been taken. Not even his laptop, still closed and on the counter where he'd left it. Even his backpack seemed to be untouched, hung on the back of one of the chairs at the kitchen table.

He held the phone up to one ear and stood in

front of the bathroom mirror to shave what was left of the three or four days' growth on his face.

When Lauren answered, he told her he'd be late for dinner but didn't go into any details about why. "I got held up," was all he said.

By the time he arrived, Lauren was at the bar with a martini in her hand. He didn't think she drank a lot, although she looked to have been more than a few into the night when he pulled up the stool next to her.

His only other thought was how good she looked in a skirt and sleeveless shirt, low cut to show off more than she ever had before. At least around him. It almost caught him by surprise and left him without words for a few seconds. In fact, he rarely saw her dress up at all, other than the time she had to appear in court with him when they were involved in a libel suit. Joe was accused of defamation of character by an accused child rapist who also happened to be the mayor in a small city northwest of Miami.

Lauren had her hair down past her shoulders and pushed a strand back from her face. She didn't even have her glasses on. Another first, as far as Joe knew. He noticed her green eyes.

"You look… unbelievable," he said. And he meant it.

She sipped her martini and smiled over the glass.

"Thank you." But then she squinted her eyes, reached into her purse, and pulled out her glasses. "Oh my God! Joe… what happened?"

Joe reached for the bruise on his eye. "Oh, this? Well…" He knew there was no hiding what had happened but didn't want her to worry. "I had a couple of visitors. That's why I was late." He turned and showed her the lump on the back of his head. "Got hit in the head with something hard. I didn't see it, but I'd guess it was a pipe or—"

"Did you call the police?"

Joe shook his head. "After I woke up, I knew I was already late. I just thought—"

"After you woke up? You were knocked out?"

Joe nodded. "For a few minutes."

"What'd they look like?"

"I don't know. I didn't get a good look at them."

She gave Joe a suspicious stare. "You wouldn't miss cross-eyes on a fly, but you're going to tell me you didn't get a good look at them?" She pulled off her glasses and placed them back in her purse."

"Can you see without those?" Joe said.

She shrugged. "Not really. But don't change the subject, Joe. What's going on here? What aren't you telling me? And why wouldn't you call the cops?"

The bartender came over and stood in front of Joe. "What're you having?"

"I'll have a vodka cranberry." He turned to Lauren. "You want another one?"

She tilted her glass and looked inside, then

puckered her lips and twisted them a bit. "Sure, why not." She picked up her glass, finished what was left, and pushed it toward the bartender.

"So now you know why I was late."

Lauren kept her eyes on him. "I thought maybe you changed your mind about our fun night out together." She turned and looked toward the tables. "We lost our reservation... but the woman at the desk said she'd see if she could get us another table. It might be a while."

"I'm sorry," Joe said.

"Don't be sorry, Joe. Jesus. I just..." She stopped and looked straight ahead. "I just wish you would tell me what this is all about. I know you too well to let you keep from telling me exactly what happened."

Joe was hesitant to tell her what he was thinking. It's not like he knew for sure, but he had a pretty good idea. "They didn't take anything. And they didn't speak a word. Roughed me up and knocked some things around. But otherwise..." He stopped mid-sentence, watched the bartender put their drinks in front of them, then picked up his drink and took a sip. "I think it was some kind of a message. Maybe a warning."

"A warning? What's that supposed to mean?"

"I'm not sure it makes a lot of sense, but I can't help but wonder if it has something to do with Matt Doyle. Someone could have told him I was looking for him."

Lauren had a look of concern on her face. She was turned toward Joe, her knees almost touching his thigh but not quite. "I thought all you had to do was find out where he was? You said it was nothing. But now, you have a couple of goons show up at your apartment?" She sipped her martini, reached in with her fingers and pulled out an olive, popped it in her mouth. "Does that mean it has to do with those names I got you?"

Joe sipped his drink and faced forward before he turned back to her. "That's exactly what I'm afraid of. The cousin, Daniel Doyle, said Matt stole his wife's diamond ring. And he had a woman with him who went by the name of Pam. But he said he was almost sure that wasn't her name."

"Pam?"

"Yeah, and this so-called Pam lady was in the bathroom with this guy's wife and apparently helped her after she was stung by a bee out on their balcony. Daniel said after Matt and his girlfriend left, his wife's ring was gone. And that's the last time he'd seen or heard from Matt."

"And he's sure they took it?"

"The ring?" Joe didn't answer her, just took another sip and gathered his thoughts. "The next place I go to is that woman, Morgan Brown's apartment."

Lauren nodded. "She was very active online."

"Turns out her sister dated Matt Doyle. She also hadn't seen either one in a while. Then she tells me her sister's dating some old man but doesn't say her name or anything. I asked if it was Pam and she said no. Of course, if that wasn't her real name to begin with…"

"What's her sister's name?"

Joe finished his vodka cranberry, wiped his mouth with the cocktail napkin. "I'm about to leave without getting much information from Morgan and see a photo on the credenza right before the door. I pick it up and sure enough recognize her sister right away." Joe had his eyes on her, watched her expression as he purposefully let the suspense build.

"Are you going to tell me who it is?"

Joe turned to the bartender and held up his empty glass. He looked back at Lauren. "Her sister is Dickie's new girlfriend. Scarlett Calise."

Lauren's eyes opened wide. "You sure? Different last names?"

"Her married name is Brown." Joe looked around the bar, kept his voice low. "Scarlett wears a diamond on her right hand. I thought maybe she was divorced or… I don't know, really. But then when I put it all together, and if she's the same woman who was with Matt…"

"She stole the diamond ring!"

Joe put his finger up to his lips and looked around. "Shhh, Dickie knows a lot of people around here. We should be quiet."

"But if his girlfriend is hanging around with this

guy Matt, then…"

Joe reached for the drink as soon as the bartender put it in front of him. "Scarlett is up to something. I didn't tell you sooner because I wanted to talk to Dickie. I met him at Mickey Cho's Water Club."

"You told him?"

"No. Not yet. I just wanted to see what else he knew about Scarlett. Turns out… not much. I also wanted to know if he'd told her I was working for him, to find this guy Matt."

"And?"

Joe shook his head. "He hasn't told her much about his business. Not more than he has to… at least that's what he told me."

"Why didn't you tell him?"

He shrugged. "There's a lot I haven't told him yet." Joe sipped his drink with his eyes on the TV. The baseball game was on—the Marlins and the Padres. "She came on to me. And I don't mean just a little flirty. I had to push her off and asked her to leave."

"Why didn't you tell him?" Lauren said.

Joe shrugged. "Not sure what good it would do. All she'd say was he'd be okay with it; they had an agreement. She even told him she was at my place having a drink. But I didn't bring it up." He shook his head. "Dickie's a nice guy until you cross him. I don't need him wondering if something happened even when nothing did."

13

JOE SLEPT WITH one eye open, out of bed well before seven. He was behind the wheel of the Mercedes, his mind running through the different scenarios of when the two thugs showed up at his apartment. He wished he'd done something more, at least rip the mask off one of them. Then he'd at least have something to tell the cops, not just that two guys walked in and kicked his ass and he barely put up a fight.

He drove into the lot at Ray's Auto Repair—Dickie's place—and parked toward the back of the lot. There were a lot of cars, but a good number of them were dead and used for show. Dickie told him one time he wanted to make the place look busier than it was, so he purchased a few truckloads of broken-down cars from the auction and kept them parked in the lot.

Joe walked toward the open garage door and saw

Colt by the front fender of an old Mustang convertible painted fire-engine red.

Colt had the hood open, his eyes on the engine and a Styrofoam cup in one hand, a cigarette in the other. He took a sip, drew from his cigarette, and blew the smoke off to the side.

Joe walked in and Colt looked past him.

"You driving that Mercedes now?"

Joe turned and looked back toward the lot. "Dickie wants me to buy it." He looked toward the closed door to the office with a sign taped to it. Big handwritten letters read, KEEP CLOSED AT ALL TIMES!!

Colt said, "Scarlett's driving a new BMW now. Not brand new, but only got a few thousand miles on it. Dickie got it from the auction, was going to sell it, but I guess she don't like the old diesel." Colt shook his head. "She gets whatever she wants." He looked at Joe and took another drag from his cigarette, dropped it on the ground and crushed it with his foot.

Joe stepped toward the door to the office, looked past the sign through the glass. "Is she here?" he said.

"Who, Scarlett?" Colt shook his head. "Haven't seen her in a few days. Normally she's here at this time, but…"

"Dickie here?"

"Not right now." Colt took another sip from his cup and turned back toward the Mustang.

Joe looked out into the lot at the front of the building, then looked back toward the rear. There was enough space for four cars, two garage doors at the back of the building and two in front. The Mustang was the only car in the garage. "Hey, Colt," he said. "Where's my car? Dickie have it junked already?"

Colt didn't respond right away. "Is that what he told you?" He scratched his cheek. "He had me make the repairs. Somebody came in yesterday looking for a cheap car, so Dickie sold it to him."

"I thought you said it wasn't worth fixing?"

"If you had to've paid for the repairs, it wasn't." He rested his cup on the Mustang's fender and leaned over the engine.

Joe couldn't believe it. He turned and walked out without another word.

He was halfway across the lot, headed back to the Mercedes, and Colt said, "You want me to tell Scarlett you were here looking for her?"

Joe looked back at him but didn't answer.

Colt stood under the open garage door and wiped his hands together with a rag. "Then you prefer I don't tell Dickie you were looking for her either?"

Joe stopped mid-step and turned back, looked at Colt with that stupid smile on his face. "What's that supposed to mean?" Joe said. He walked up to Colt and stood just a few feet away and looked him straight in the eye. "I don't like what you're implying, Colt."

Colt dropped the smile from his face. "Jesus, Joe. Take it easy. I'm just messing around, man."

Joe drove out to Miami Lakes, pulled the Mercedes into the parking lot and parked next to Will's Jeep. Joe looked inside when he walked past it toward Will's building, noticed what looked like a pile of parking tickets held stacked together with a rubber band and stuck between the driver's seat and the console.

With a tall to-go cup of coffee in each hand, he backed into the glass door, and took the stairs. He stopped on the third floor, grabbed the door's handle with his pinky without putting the coffee down and pulled it open the rest of the way with his foot.

He walked along the long hall until he got to Will's office. This time the door was closed. He leaned into it without a free hand to knock and said, "Will? You in there?"

From the other side of the door, Will said, "Yeah, just give me a minute, all right?"

Joe waited, and almost put the coffee on the floor in the hall so he could try the knob. "Will? Would you mind opening the door? My hands are full."

The door opened. Will held his hand on the edge of the door and stood in the doorway. His shirt was untucked. His hair went up in all directions.

Joe stood outside in the hall, reached out toward

Will with one of the coffees. "Here. Are you going to let me in?"

Will grabbed the cup and backed away from the door. "Thanks, Joe. I was just going to go out and grab a cup."

Joe stepped inside and his eyes went to the blanket and pillow folded up in the corner on the floor. "Did you sleep here?"

Will sat behind his desk and glanced at the pillow and blanket as if there was nothing to it. He pointed with his thumb. "What? No, I just got here early and… real early… working on a case. I keep that stuff here in case I'm on an all-nighter, or…"

"I called your apartment," Joe said. "Your message didn't come on. I don't remember the last time I called a number without voicemail." He stared back at Will, but Will looked down at his desk. "Is everything all right, Will?" He sat in the chair in front of the desk.

Will looked past him, out into the hall. "Yeah. Everything's good. Real good."

"You sure?"

Will picked up the coffee, cracked the plastic cover and took a sip. "I appreciate the coffee, Joe." He paused. "This working for yourself thing, it's not as easy as they make it sound, you know."

They both sat quiet.

Joe said, "If you needed work, then why'd you give me such a hard time about helping me with Dickie?"

Will turned and looked at the pillow and blanket, left his gaze there for a couple of moments before he finally turned back to Joe. "Did you tell Dickie I was going to help you?"

Joe shook his head. "No. I'm supposed to keep it quiet for now. I just thought it'd be best that I—"

"I owe Dickie money."

Joe leaned forward in the chair. He knew what Will said but hoped he'd heard wrong. "You what? Did you say you owe Dickie money?"

"I actually thought maybe that's why you came out to see me the other day." He let out a nervous laugh. "It's not actually Dickie I owe. I mean, it sort of is. But, really, it's an associate of his. He wouldn't take my money on a bet if I wrapped it up in gold and put a bow on top."

Joe sat quiet, listening.

The forced smile Will had kept on his face disappeared. "He turned me on to this other guy, told me if I pulled any shit I'd be in trouble with him. I'm glad Dickie didn't send you."

"He wouldn't ask me to do that." Joe looked into his cup. "How much?"

"How much?"

Joe nodded. "Will, just tell me, will you? How much do you owe?"

Will brushed his hand through the air toward Joe. "Ah, it's nothing." He turned and looked toward the window. "Twenty grand."

"Twenty grand? Jesus Christ, Will. That's not

nothing." He looked into the corner behind Will's desk. "Where's your camera equipment?"

Will followed Joe's eyes and looked behind him. "Oh, I, uh… I sold it."

"How are you going to do your work without your camera?"

"Oh, I'm looking at some options. I don't need all that high-end equipment just to shoot some asshole working out in the gym with an injury claim."

Joe thought for a moment. "I told you I'll split the money with you. Of course, now I definitely won't tell Dickie you're helping me. But it doesn't matter. We'll split it down the middle." He looked Will in the eye. "Don't go selling stuff, Will."

Will gave Joe a serious look. "I don't need your charity, Joe. You're the one working for that rinky-dink newspaper, if you can even call it that." He held his hands out and looked around his office. "Look at me. I'm the one with my own company." He closed his eyes and shook his head. "Who am I kidding. You're right, Joe. I'm broke. I don't have a goddamn dime to my name." He looked up and across the desk. "You don't have to give me half. But I'd appreciate the work." He cracked a smile. "I've always missed working together."

14

JOE HAD LEARNED how to shoot a gun way back but hadn't picked one up in quite a few years. He spent quite a bit of time at the shooting range when he was a young reporter writing a column about how easy it was to get your hands on a gun in America.

Times hadn't changed much since then.

He was on Southwest Eighth Street and pulled in front of La Estrella de Plata, which was Spanish for The Silver Star. It was a place just south of Little Havana that'd once been the go-to place to buy a gun. Although they sold everything else pawned too.

Joe could've gone anywhere he wanted, but it'd been a while since he saw Juan Pedro De Capella, the shop's owner.

Juan was behind the counter when Joe walked in, sipping from a tall, narrow coffee mug with his eyes on the *Calle Ocho News*. His reading glasses on the edge of his nose, he pulled them off and looked toward the door. It took him a moment to say a word, then a smile took over his face. "Aaayyyy, Jose!" He tucked his glasses into his shirt pocket and walked around the glass-top counter, held his arms out, and gave Joe a hug. "It's been too long, my friend." He eased up on the hug and took a step back, looked Joe over. "You got a little older, my friend." He clenched his fists and curled his arms out in front of him. "But you still have all that muscle." He nodded. "Ju wanna café?"

Joe shook his head. "No, I'm good. But how are things, Juan? Everything good?" His eyes went toward the display case with at least a few dozen pistols behind the glass, then up toward the rack behind the counter with the shotguns and rifles.

"I can't complain, my friend. Can't complain." He shrugged. "I'm still alive." He walked around to the other side of the display case and picked up his mug, took a sip, and gave Joe a nod. "So what do I owe the pleasure?"

Joe scratched his head and looked around, nodded toward a large, framed photo of Barbara Streisand, poster-size, hung up on the wall. "Is that for sale?"

"Everything's for sale, my friend. You want the clothes off my back? Make me an offer." He laughed, sipped from his mug, and looked at Joe from over the rim.

"Seriously," Joe said. "How much?"

Juan walked toward it, pulled the bottom of the frame away from the wall. He looked at the tag. "Fifty dollars. But for you? I'll take sixty." He laughed, shook his head and said, "You give me forty dollars, it's yours." He looked up at the picture. "I don't even know who she is."

Joe stepped toward the display case and looked at the guns. He recognized some of them, although he was far from an expert on guns. He watched Juan pull the framed poster down off the wall and take it around to the other side of the counter.

Juan pulled a key from his pocket and opened the glass case from the other side. He slid the back open and looked up at Joe. "Which one you like?"

Joe crouched and looked at them through the glass. "Nothing too big. But powerful enough nobody'll get up if I have to use it." He looked up at Juan. "Something for protection," he said. He stood up and looked at the racks on the wall behind Juan. "What are those?"

Juan closed the back of the case and dropped the keys in his pocket. He turned to the wall behind him, then looked across the counter at Joe and waited.

"Maybe a pistol of some sort to keep on me. Keep a shotgun in the trunk."

Juan pulled his keys from his pocket again and opened the back of the case. He reached inside and pulled out a gun, placed it in front of Joe. "It's a Glock 19. Almost brand new."

Joe picked it up, held it and moved his hand up and down to get a feel for the weight.

Juan kept his eye on the gun in Joe's hand. "It is easy to use, my friend. You want protection?" He nodded once toward the Glock 19. "This will do the job."

Joe looked up toward the racks behind Juan and pointed. "What's that one there, third from the left."

Juan took the Glock from Joe and locked it in the case. He turned and looked at the wall. "The Mossberg?" He glanced at Joe over his shoulder. "You won't fit this in your pants, I'm afraid." He pulled it from the rack and placed it on the glass.

Joe grabbed it, held it in one hand.

Juan said, "12-gauge, weighs about seven pounds."

Joe ran his eyes along the barrel, looked up at Juan.

Juan cracked a slight smile. "He won't get up, you hit him with that." He turned and pointed toward the rack. "You want to see the 20-gauge? Same gun, less recoil."

Joe shook his head. "No, I like this one. I'll take it." He looked into the display case between them. "And I'll take the Glock, too." He leaned forward and looked down at the floor behind Juan. "And don't forget the Barbara Streisand poster."

Joe stood to the side, just outside Morgan Brown's

door. He looked back and forth along the hall and almost knocked a third time but stopped when he heard a sound from the other side. He leaned into the door with his ear and listened.

It was a woman's voice. Not loud, but he had no doubt there was someone there. He knocked. "Morgan? It's Joe Sheldon."

He kept his eye on the knob but it didn't move. He waited, then knocked again. "Morgan?"

He wished he had the Glock on him, but even though Juan had known him all those years, the laws were stricter than they were in the old days. He had to wait.

The door clicked twice, then opened.

Morgan stood in the doorway. Joe looked over her shoulder and, sure enough, behind her, stood her sister Scarlett.

Morgan glanced at him. "I'm sorry, Joe."

"Can I come in?" he said.

Morgan stepped back from the door and Joe walked inside. He stared back at Scarlett and didn't say a word.

"Aren't you going to say hello?" Scarlett said, gave him half a smile.

Joe sniffed, smelled the marijuana in the air. "I guess you're both talking again?" He turned to Scarlett. "You want to tell me where your boyfriend is?"

She held her gaze on him. "Dickie?"

He shook his head. "Don't play games with me.

Okay? You know who I'm talking about." He stared at Scarlett. "Matt Doyle?"

Scarlett shook her head. "I don't know where you heard he was my boyfriend." She turned from him and walked toward the glass balcony doors at the far end of the room. With her back to him, she said, "That's all in the past."

Joe took a couple of steps toward her. "Then why keep it a secret?"

She turned to Joe. "What secret? Am I supposed to tell you my life's history? Just because you're a friend of Dickie's?"

Joe kept his eyes on her. "Do I look like an idiot?" He stood between Morgan and Scarlett, shifted his eyes from one to the other. "I'd rather not play games, if it's all right with the two of you?"

Scarlett shrugged. "There's nothing I can do if you don't believe me." She picked up her purse from the back of a wooden chair pushed up against the wall. She threw it on her shoulder and walked past Joe, toward the door.

Joe looked at Morgan. "She's leaving?"

Morgan didn't answer.

Scarlett left without another word, and Morgan leaned her back up against the door, preventing Joe from going after her.

"What are you doing?" he said. He tried to reach for the knob.

"Let her go," she said.

"Let her go? I just wanted to talk to her."

Morgan folded her arms at her chest, her back still against the door. "She doesn't know where Matt is."

Joe looked her in the eye. "Can you please step out of my way?"

Morgan shook her head and cracked a slight smile, playing a game. "Why don't you make me?"

15

JOE PARKED THE Mercedes on the cobblestone driveway in front of Dickie's house, stepped out and walked along the pathway past the fountain with the concrete dolphin spraying water from its mouth.

Joe had barely gotten to the front door when it opened and Dickie stepped out onto the top step.

"You son of a bitch!" Dickie said, his thick and hairy short arms folded in front of him. The gold bracelet dangled from his wrist. "She told me everything."

Joe stopped before the bottom step and looked up at Dickie. "I have no idea what you're talking about."

"Don't play dumb with me, Joey. I'm no fool."

Joe shook his head. "Dickie, I mean it. I don't know what you're—"

"You've made her very upset."

"Okay, Dickie. This doesn't make any sense. If

she told you I saw her at her sister's apartment, then I hope she told you why I was there."

"You can't stand the fact you don't have anyone, but here I am… with a beautiful young woman, who—"

"Did she tell you she knows who Matt Doyle is?"

Dickie looked off, still shaking his head as if he hadn't heard a word. "You come on to the woman I love? Behind my back? How could you, Joey? How could you?"

Joe's eyes bugged out of his head. "What? She told you I came on to her? Are you kidding me?"

"You expect me to believe you didn't put the moves on her?" He looked down the steps. "I know how you are, Joey. Act all cool and quiet around the ladies, then you make your move. And here I am, I really believed we were friends."

"Dickie. Christ, you're serious? She's lying to you. Just like she'll lie to you when you ask her about Matt Doyle. Why do you think she never mentioned his name to you? Well, I'll tell you why. Because they're up to something. You think it's just a coincidence you end up with her, and now you're looking for a guy who stiffed you ninety grand?"

Dickie shook his head. "She already told me she dated him. She said if I'd only been honest with her, told her I was looking for him, she might've been able to help. But she hasn't seen him since the holidays."

Joe closed his eyes and shook his head, looked

along the walkway and scratched his head. He looked up at his friend. "She's playing you, Dickie. I'm telling you."

Dickie narrowed his eyes, let his arms hang by his side. He pointed toward the street. "I want you off my property. Right now." His eyes shifted toward the Mercedes. "And leave the car. It doesn't belong to you."

"What? Are you serious? What am I supposed to do, walk home from here?" Joe turned when he heard a car pull in the driveway behind him.

Scarlett pulled in driving her white BMW, drove around the Mercedes and stopped.

Joe said, "Good. Now we can get this straightened out." He waited for Scarlett to step out of the car.

"You leave her alone," Dickie said. "And I told you I want you to leave. That means now." He waved toward Scarlett, still seated behind the wheel. "Come on, sweetie. He's leaving."

She opened the door and Joe walked toward her.

Dickie came down the steps and grabbed him by the arm. "I told you to leave her alone."

Joe yanked his arm from Dickie's grasp and continued toward Scarlett. "You told him I came on to you?"

Scarlett walked past him without making eye contact, went over and stood next to Dickie. "Your friend's a liar," she said, then shifted her eyes to Joe. "You're going to look your friend in the eye, tell him you didn't kiss me?" She stared back at him with a look on her face like she wanted to smile but held it in.

Joe wasn't sure what to say. He looked from Scarlett to Dickie, opened his mouth to defend himself but stopped.

Dickie put his arm around Scarlett's shoulder and she looked at him, smiled, and kissed him on the cheek. They both turned and walked toward the steps, but Scarlett turned and looked back at Joe, gave him a devious smile.

Dickie went up the stairs to the front door, Scarlett under his arm, and turned to Joe. "I'm not going to make you walk, Joe. You keep the car. But you'll need to pay me in full." He opened the door and let Scarlett walk in ahead of him, then closed the door.

Joe walked into the building where he worked and into the office. He stopped just inside the doorway and looked around. He wondered why the place was so quiet.

Lauren had her eyes on the computer screen in front of her. She didn't seem to notice he'd walked in at first. But she removed her earbuds and looked up at Joe. She looked toward the owner's office. "Ralph is looking for you."

Joe looked through the glass at Ralph Connor, the owner of the rag for the last thirty years. Ralph was on the phone and looked the other way when he turned toward Joe.

Joe said to Lauren, "Where is everyone?"

"Ralph will tell you." She rolled her seat back from the desk and looked up at Joe. "It's not good."

"What's 'not good'?" Joe watched her until she looked away, fixed her eyes back on the computer screen.

"Just go see him," she said.

He looked toward Ralph's office again, saw he was off the phone. He walked toward the door and knocked.

"Come in," Ralph said.

Joe turned the knob and looked back at Lauren before he stepped inside. "You wanted to see me?"

Ralph leaned back in his chair. "Close the door." He pointed toward the two chairs in front of the desk and Joe sat across from him.

The office was small and somewhat cramped with a big desk that didn't fit. But the windows on the walls facing everyone else on the other side of the glass made it feel bigger than it was.

Joe looked at the plant Ralph had on top of the filing cabinet behind his desk, with the brown and yellow leaves. He wondered how long it had been since it was watered.

Ralph leaned forward on the desk and played with a pen between both hands. "I loved your last column," he said. "You know, when I started this paper forty years ago, I thought all I wanted to do was be a writer. I wasn't good enough to get in with the big papers. In fact, I couldn't get a job anywhere. So I borrowed some money, bought this rag—and the building—for next to nothing."

Joe waited, quiet. He watched Ralph's hands fiddle with the gold pen.

Ralph had his eyes back down on the pen. "But it didn't take me long to realize what everyone else already knew. I had to be honest with myself." He lifted his eyes to Joe. "I wasn't much of a writer." He sniffed out a slight laugh. "But I was good at making money."

"I've seen your writing. I think you're being a little hard on yourself."

Ralph put his palm up toward Joe. "Let me finish, okay?" He smiled, lips tight together. He looked out through the window toward where Lauren sat by herself. All the other desks were empty. "The one thing I couldn't do was keep up with the technology and compete with the big boys out there. Even to stay local…" He turned and picked up the newspaper from the shelf behind him. "This business was built on paper. And although our customers are still willing to pay to have what turns out to be old news before it's even delivered…" He shook his head, tossed the paper on the desk. "I just thought if I had the talent, guys like you on my staff, we could be better than good. We could be great. And when you were let go from the *Post*…"

"I wasn't 'let go' from the *Post*, Ralph. I—"

"Okay, well, whatever you want to call it. I'm just telling you, it was a blessing to me. All the years I wanted to make this paper something more. I knew I couldn't do it without real talent." He had his eyes out the window again. "You and Lauren, you both just fell in my lap. I knew I couldn't pay you what you deserved. But you were the stars I needed at the time."

Joe didn't like the way he said that. *At the time.*

Ralph's eyes widened. "No disrespect to the rest of the staff. Tony and Branden. And Melissa. They're decent writers. But you... you were the answer to my dreams." His eyes went down to the pen in his hands. He placed it on the desk.

Joe knew Ralph liked to stretch his stories out. Beat around the bush. Even if he wasn't a great writer, he knew how to build suspense.

Joe leaned forward in the chair, his elbows rested on his thighs. "Ralph, can you tell me where you're going with all this?"

"I'm sorry, Joe. I thought the buy-in would give me the cash we needed. I'd hoped to retire, leave this place in good hands and make sure it didn't die whenever I did."

It took Joe some time, but he'd started to add it all up. The office was empty, and it was well past lunch. And Ralph wasn't his usual animated self. "Ralph, I appreciate all you've said. But can you just tell me what the hell's going on?"

Ralph looked down and stayed quiet. When he

looked back up at Joe, he had tears in his eyes. "When I sold such a big share, they assured me we'd have the money we needed to keep it running." He shook his head and looked Joe in the eye. "They're closing us down. I don't mean the whole paper. It'll still be here. But it'll be run out of some place in Texas; they run hundreds of local papers just like this one, and—"

"I'm fired?"

Ralph shook his head. "I wouldn't say you're fired, but… we're all done here. All of us. They want me out, too."

Joe shook his head. "No, Ralph. You just don't *have* to work anymore. You sold out. You're the one who got all the money. It's the rest of us…" Joe looked out toward Lauren through the glass. Her eyes were still on her computer screen.

"I took the money because they'd promised to turn this paper into something I couldn't do myself. I never imagined they'd…" Ralph paused. "I'm sorry, Joe. I really am."

"Is there at least a severance package? Or are we just out on the street?"

Ralph didn't answer, but Joe knew the truth.

"Jesus Christ, Ralph. You couldn't even get us a little something? I mean… what am I supposed to do now? Who's going to hire *me* to write?"

"I tried to get them to keep you on board. You and Lauren. But they said you make too much."

"Too much?" Joe laughed. "Ralph, nothing

personal but you didn't pay me shit. You promised me more money, and I'd hoped when you sold a piece of the business that'd be the answer. I never imagined I'd be out of work."

"They hire kids, Joe. Kids straight out of school. Shit, I don't even know if they're here in the US. The way these guys operate, wouldn't surprise me if the stuff's written in some Third World country."

16

JOE AND LAUREN sat at the bar at Jack's Hideaway in South Beach. It was somewhat of a dive but a perfect place to have drinks away from the other pretentious restaurants.

Lauren's eyes shifted around. Joe knew it wasn't exactly her kind of place.

"You all right?" he said.

She sipped her martini. "Haven't been in a place like this in years, to be honest."

Joe smiled and sipped his drink, finished what was left. "Hard to beat Eddie's. Good food, cheap drinks, it's a hidden gem."

The bartender walked over and took Joe's empty glass without asking, replaced it with a fresh vodka cranberry.

Joe turned to Lauren. "Reggie, this is Lauren."

Reggie pulled the towel off his shoulder and wiped his hand, reached out, and shook Lauren's.

"Nice to meet you." He turned back to Joe. "How's the day going for both of you?"

Joe hesitated. "I guess you could say it's *going*?"

The bartender didn't respond or ask any more questions. He wasn't the type of guy to get deep in conversation and knew when to walk away. He gave Lauren a nod. "Another dirty martini?"

She didn't answer.

Joe looked at her. "One more?"

She nodded toward Reggie. "Thanks." Lauren looked around the bar, not very busy except for a couple of young men playing darts in the far corner. She turned to Joe, on her stool, her elbow resting on the edge of the bar. "You seem more relaxed than I thought you'd be," she said.

Joe sipped his drink, and Reggie put the dirty martini in front of Lauren.

"Thank you," she said.

"I was upset at first, of course. I wouldn't say I'm happy about it. And I certainly don't like the idea of having to go back out and pound the pavement." He shrugged. "But it's not like he paid us much."

Lauren picked up the martini and took a sip. "Good thing you have the work you're doing for Dickie." She took another sip and turned back to face the bar. "Good for both of us, right?"

Joe didn't want to tell her what had happened. But he knew he had to. "Yeah, about that... it sort of fell through."

Lauren looked at him funny. "Fell *through*? What's

that supposed to mean?"

"It hasn't been a good day for me all around," he said. But he didn't want to go into details. He wasn't sure where to begin. "His girlfriend, Scarlett, told him I came on to her. She told him I kissed her." He sipped his drink without looking at Lauren.

"Did you?" she said.

"No. She's just making it up because she needs to keep Dickie away from me, make sure he won't trust me."

"Didn't you tell him her boyfriend was Matt Doyle?"

"She'd already told him before I got there," Joe said. "There was no surprise at all. Dickie just defended her, like it's just a goddamn coincidence the guy who stiffed him is connected to his girlfriend."

"Didn't you just tell him it wasn't true? That you'd never make a move on your friend's girlfriend?"

Joe didn't answer.

Lauren shook her head. "Oh no. Don't tell me you—"

"No! I swear, I didn't do a thing." He looked away. "She kissed me. She showed up at my apartment. Late. She threw herself at me."

"You kissed her?"

Joe had to think through his words before they came out of his mouth. "She kissed *me*. I had to throw her off of me, shoved her tongue down my throat, and—"

"And you couldn't lie to Dickie. Because she said you kissed her, you couldn't even deny it?" She shook her head and let out a slight laugh. "Joe, this would be one of those times it might be all right to lie. Just a little."

"I wish I had. She just… the whole thing caught me off guard."

"If you just tell him the truth, Joe. He'll listen to you. You know he will."

Joe sipped his drink. "I don't know. It's different now. It's like she's got a goddamn spell on him."

"Yeah, it's called having a young, hot blonde sleeping in your bed. A spell any horny old man would fall under." She put her hand on Joe's leg but then pulled it away like she hadn't meant to do it.

They both exchanged a look.

Joe held up his empty glass to Reggie and looked at Lauren's glass, but she'd hardly made a dent. "I didn't want to break the guy's heart either. He's in love with her. I know he gets his rocks off and all, but he's in love with her. I just… I need to be sure before I ruin that for him."

"Ruin it? She showed up at your door and tried to seduce you, Joe. I think he deserves to know the truth."

Reggie put another vodka cranberry on the bar, took the cash from in front of Joe, rang it up in the register, and put a few coins back down.

Joe looked straight ahead, the glass in his hand and both elbows up on the bar. "It's not like there's a lot of women waiting to have sex with a short, chubby, old man. Not unless he's paying."

"He is paying," Lauren said. "He's got a lot of money. Why else would this bimbo be with him? It's not like it's his personality."

Joe shrugged. "Like I said, I need to be sure. And if I can prove she's up to something with this guy Matt Doyle…"

"But I thought you said it fell through? He still wants you to—"

"He didn't say. I just assumed the deal was dead." He sipped his drink and turned to Lauren. "He told me to give his car back. Wanted me to leave it there. But then I guess he felt bad, told me to keep it. I just have to pay him in full somehow."

"He owes you something," she said. "Doesn't he? You did the work. You tracked the guy down, at least have some pretty strong leads, right?"

Joe said, "Dickie wouldn't pay someone for an incomplete job. I can guarantee that."

They both faced the bar and sat quiet.

Lauren turned to him. "Then why don't you finish the job? Prove his girlfriend's up to no good. Or at least prove to him you're not the bad guy. I know you don't want to break his heart, but…"

He shrugged. "I don't know. Maybe I'll let things cool off for a few days, see if he'll talk to me."

"Why wait?" she said. "What if we find Matt Doyle? Bring him to Dickie's door, tell him to pay up?" She sipped her martini and looked at him over the rim. "I promised Ralph I'd finish the project I was working on, but there's not much left to do. So, I'm free to help, as much as you need me to."

Joe had a good buzz and thought back to the apartment, when he smoked the joint with Scarlett's sister.

"I bought a couple of guns," he said.

Lauren looked surprised. "What kinds of guns?"

"A shotgun and a Glock pistol." He picked up his glass and held it in his hand, the bottom rested on his thigh. "For protection, in case those two goons show up again."

"A shotgun? You're going to carry a shotgun around?"

Joe shrugged. "Thought I'd keep it in my trunk."

17

JOE PULLED INTO the parking lot outside Will's office. He stepped out of the Mercedes and his phone rang. He didn't recognize the number. And when he answered, the last person he'd expected on the other end was Morgan.

"I just wanted to apologize for the other day," she said.

Joe said, "I get it. She's your sister. But now she's up to something, trying to get me to stop looking for Matt Doyle. Told Dickie I kissed her, and—"

"She told me the same thing."

Joe raised his voice. "I didn't kiss her!" He looked around the parking lot and eased his tone back a bit. "Why is she telling people that? If you want the truth, she kissed *me*. I had to throw her out of my apartment."

"Well, that's between you and Scarlett. But that's not what I'm calling about," she said. "I'm concerned. Scarlett said she wasn't hanging around with Matt anymore, but I'm not sure I believe her. I should've just let you talk to her."

"I didn't think you'd trust me." He looked in through the glass doors toward the lobby of the building.

"You seem like a good person. Maybe I'm wrong." The line went quiet.

"So, you're calling to apologize? Or is there more to it?"

"I asked Scarlett about Matt. She said she hadn't even talked to him. But I don't believe her. She's hiding something."

Joe nodded into the phone. "You're not telling me anything I don't know."

Morgan was quiet. "He has a friend, owns some apartments in South Miami. Scarlett drove down there yesterday. I don't know what she was doing, but if I had to guess…"

"Doyle lives there?"

"I don't know. I followed her."

Joe thought for a moment. "You lied when you said you hadn't talked to her in months. So why would I believe you now?"

"What did you want me to tell you? A stranger shows up at my door asking about my sister's ex-boyfriend. I mean, we're nowhere as close as we used to be. So it's not like she tells me everything going on in her life. I've never even met the old man she's sleeping with."

"Dickie."

"And you said he's a friend of yours? That's how you knew Scarlett, right?"

"We *were* friends. Until she told him I tried to kiss her."

The line went quiet again.

I looked around the parking lot. "Is there something you want from me?" I said. "I have to go meet a friend of mine."

"I'm afraid she's going to get herself hurt if she's hanging around with Matt again."

"But you don't know if she's with him. I mean, you didn't see him. Did you?"

"No. And I've tried calling her, but she won't answer her phone. I don't know if she's afraid to talk to me or—"

"What's the friend's name? The one who owns the apartments?"

"Idél. I don't know his last name. He's a creepy little thing."

"Creepy?"

"Yeah. He's about five feet tall. Maybe a little bigger. I'm five nine, and not sure he comes up to my chin."

"You know him?"

"No. Saw him once. That was enough. The way his nose is pushed up into his face..." She let out somewhat of a snort. "I'm not even sure he's all human. Poor thing."

"Do you have the address?"

"The address?"

"To the apartment building this guy Idél owns."

"I'm not sure. It's off Southwest Seventy-First. I can get you the exact address if you want?"

"I'll find it. The guy's name is Idél. Spelled I-D-E-L?"

"I think so."

Will walked out of the building and gave Joe a nod. "Sorry, I was finishing up a couple of things.

They walked together toward the Mercedes, and Joe slid the key in the passenger side, unlocked the door for Will. "I'm not trying to be romantic or anything. It won't unlock from the inside." He walked around to the driver's side and looked at Will across the roof. "I got you a camera. Got a one-fifty to three hundred millimeter zoom."

They both stepped inside the car.

Will turned to him. "You bought me a camera? What the hell for?"

"Because you're going to help me, aren't you? And if you don't have a camera…"

Will stared back at Joe from the passenger seat. "But you just told me you lost your job. You probably oughta be careful with your money." He looked straight ahead through the windshield. "Take it from me. I don't know how much you have saved, but…"

"I got it cheap, went to see Juan." Joe stuck his

key in the ignition and turned over the engine. He reached in back and grabbed the camera, handed it to Will. "It's not the best, but…"

Will took it from Joe and looked over the Canon. "You spend a lot?"

Joe shrugged. "Two hundred even."

Will's eyes widened. "No shit? The lens is worth twice that." He looked the camera over some more. "I'll pay you back."

Joe shook his head. "I don't want you to pay me back. I just want you to help me." He shifted into drive and pulled out onto the street, turned onto 826.

"If Dickie doesn't want you looking for this guy, then why are we going down there?"

Joe kept his eyes on the road. "I've known Dickie a long time. He can be a little oversensitive, needs a little time to calm down."

"You think he'll pay you?"

Joe nodded. "If we find Matt Doyle, he will." His eyes went to the camera in Will's hand. "Get pictures, show him proof we know where he is. He's going to honor his end of the deal. That's how Dickie is."

"Even though you kissed his girlfriend?"

Joe shot Will a quick look. "Christ. I didn't kiss her." He turned his eyes back to the road, shaking his head. "And if you're up for it, if we think we can do it without putting ourselves in any kind of danger, we deliver Matt to Dickie's front door, and

—"

"Deliver him?" Will kept his eyes on Joe. "Are you serious?"

Joe gave Will a quick glance but didn't answer, turned his eyes back toward the highway.

18

JOE TOOK THE Sunset Drive exit off the Palmetto Expressway, turned left onto Southwest Fifty-Ninth Place, then onto Southwest Seventy-First.

Lauren had helped Joe find the property owned by Idél Del Rio and did a little digging into his background, told Joe he was from Cuba and made money as a professional wrestler, then invested everything he had in real estate throughout southern parts of Florida.

"Is that it?" Will said, his eyes up toward the building on the corner of Southwest Seventy-Fourth Terrace.

Joe parked on the side of the street in front of the building, counted eight floors of apartments with balconies overlooking two in-ground pools, side by side, with a fenced area surrounded by sabal palmettos.

There was a second building similar to the taller one, with the same architecture, but only three stories high. It had the same balconies but not much of a view.

"Which building?" Will said.

Joe leaned over the wheel and looked up at the buildings. "It's those two buildings. They're both owned by this guy Idél."

Will looked toward the sign on the corner. "Mayan Town Villa?" He lifted the camera, adjusted the lens, and shot a picture. He put down the window and hung the camera out, pointed it up toward the top of the building and clicked the shutter release. He turned the camera over and looked at the digital display on the back. "Not bad."

Joe said, "The lens all right?"

"As long as I'm not too far away, it should do the job."

Joe ducked his head and looked past Will, tried to see past the palmettos and the tall fence surrounding the pool area. There were plenty of people out there from what he could see. "I wonder what the people're like in a place like this." He leaned over for the glove box and pulled out the Glock.

"Where'd you get a gun?" Will said.

"Picked it up today, on the way to your office. That's when I saw the camera."

"You didn't have to wait?"

Joe pushed open the door. "I already did." He

stepped outside and tucked the gun in his pants. He closed the door, careful not to slam it.

Will stepped out from the passenger side and onto the sidewalk in front of the building. "Not like it used to be. Juan does it all by the books now?"

Joe kept his voice low and nodded toward the trunk. "Got a 12-gauge too."

Will shook his head. "I was thinking maybe I should pick something up. But you know me." He held up his camera. "I'd rather shoot this."

Joe walked up next to him on the sidewalk and headed toward the pool area. "I don't know if I care to have to use it, but I'd say it makes me feel a little more secure."

They were close, but Joe put his arm up in front of Will when they got to a row of shrubs. "This is good; we don't want anyone to see us. And I'd have to guess if Dickie's girlfriend's still in touch with Doyle. He might have an idea what I look like."

"You want me to just shoot some pictures? See what we get?"

Joe looked back at his car. "Shit, I forgot the binoculars I picked up from Juan. Let me go grab 'em."

Will said, "I think I could get a little closer. He has no idea what I look like."

Joe pulled out his phone and held it up in front of Will. "This is him. You see him, get a picture. But don't do anything else. Just be cool."

"What about the wrestler?"

"Idél? He owns the place. I can't imagine he'd be hanging around the residents." Joe turned and walked back to the Mercedes, slid his key in the trunk and popped it open. He eyed the 12-gauge packed inside the hard-shell case Juan threw in for another twenty. He closed the trunk's lid and headed back toward where he'd left Will.

But Will had already moved closer to the pool and stood just outside the fence between a couple of palmettos.

Joe stopped when a uniformed man walked up behind Will.

Joe felt the Glock in his pants and looked around, then ducked behind the shrubs. He watched Will turn around, say something to the man, but Joe couldn't hear what it was.

Will's head jerked forward as the man ripped the camera out of his hand, the strap still around Will's neck. Will fell against the trunk of the palmetto.

Joe jumped out from behind the shrub and ran toward them. "Hey! Hey! What the hell do you think you're doing?" He hurried over and helped Will to his feet.

The man turned to Joe. He had a thick neck and shoulders like a linebacker, the camera in his hand. He pulled his sunglasses from his eyes, tucked them into his shirt pocket, and stepped up to Joe.

Will stepped between them and tried to grab the camera. "Give me that, buddy."

But the man's big hand stayed wrapped around it

tight. He wouldn't let go. He gave Will a shove into Joe.

Joe pushed Will out of the way and stood chest to chest with the man. "We're with the newspaper… doing a column on pool safety at apartments throughout Miami." He looked up toward the building. "Idél told us it'd be all right if we—"

"Get off the property," the man said before Joe could finish. "Now."

Will pointed toward the pool. "Doyle's down there. I just saw him." He reached for the camera. "I have a picture."

The man pulled the camera back from Will's grip and got it free. He lifted it up over his head and smashed it on the concrete walkway where they stood.

Without a second thought Joe cocked his fist and hit the guy in the jaw.

The man stumbled back a couple of feet but shook it off. He wiped his jaw with the back of his hand. He shoved Will out of the way, turned and wrapped his thick hands around Joe's neck.

With both hands, Joe tried to pull the man's hands away. But before he could do a thing, the man let go with one hand and used it to punch Joe in the head.

Joe's legs gave out from under him. He dropped to one knee, but he came up with his shoulder and drove it into the man's groin. He sent him back into Will and knocked them both to the ground.

Joe looked toward the pool and saw a decent

crowd watching the commotion from the other side of the fence. And past the small crowd he saw Matt Doyle seated in a lounge chair with a drink in his hand.

Doyle looked directly at Joe and they locked eyes. He jumped up from his chair and ran in the other direction.

Joe started to run after Doyle, but the big man grabbed him by the shoulder. Joe turned and threw a solid punch and caught him in the jaw.

The man stumbled back, and Will jumped on top of him from behind. He yelled at Joe. "Go get him!"

Joe looked past the crowd and saw Doyle jump the fence barefoot on the other side of the pool. He ran along the fence and looked for an opening to the gate, but by the time he saw one, Doyle was already on the other side.

Doyle was a good fifty yards ahead. He ran over the grass and onto the sidewalk and continued along Seventy-Fourth Terrace.

The prick was fast even in his bare feet and practically naked in his skimpy-little-flowered bathing suit. He turned the corner onto Fifty-Ninth.

Joe pulled his Glock from his pants, had no intention of firing a shot at Doyle but thought maybe he could fire one in the air, make the guy think. He ran as fast as he could, breathing heavy and turned onto Fifty-Ninth, far behind Matt Doyle. He raised the gun. And as soon as he did, he heard a gunshot and stopped, ducked with his hands over his head.

Joe was afraid someone had fired at him. But that wasn't the case at all. And as soon as he turned and looked up the street at the apartment building, he had a bad feeling. He felt it in his gut. He turned and stared down Fifty-Ninth.

Matt Doyle was gone. Nowhere in sight.

Joe started back toward the apartment building, tucked the Glock back in his pants, then started to pick up the pace even though he was already out of breath. Sweat poured down his face, his hair over his eyes.

He slowed when he got to Seventy-Fourth and turned up the walkway toward the apartment building. He looked past the palmettos toward the pool area, but other than a couple of women drying themselves off with towels, there was nobody there. The pool area was empty. The lounge chairs were all empty.

Joe walked along the fence and looked over toward where he'd left Will and the man he assumed was some kind of security guard, although his uniform was generic, no patches or stitching or even a name.

He spotted the crowd who'd moved from the pool to just outside the fence. Something was definitely wrong. He picked up his pace and ran along the fence outside the pool until he got to the crowd of people standing shoulder to shoulder, where he and Will had fought the man.

Joe tried to get through the crowd. "Will? Will? Where are you?" He pushed his way past the wet and nearly naked bodies, stepped over the broken pieces from the shattered camera and between two women who watched him.

A woman was crouched over Will, her hand under his head.

Blood covered the concrete and ran into the grass.

Joe got down on one knee next to the woman. "Will?"

Will's eyes were closed, his Hawaiian shirt drenched in blood.

Joe put his hand on Will's shoulder. His stomach was up in his throat. "Will?"

The woman turned and stared at Joe. "He's your friend?"

Joe didn't answer, looked her in the eye. "Is he…" He couldn't finish.

She looked up at him and nodded. "I'm sorry."

19

LAUREN HAD A tissue balled up in one hand with her arms wrapped around the back of Joe's neck and pulled him tight enough he had a tough time trying to breathe.

Joe felt her wet tears drip onto his shoulder and tried to catch his breath.

"I don't understand how it happened," she said through her choking sobs. She finally eased up on him and pulled him by the hand from the door, closed it and walked into the other room. She picked up an open book from the couch and sat down, slipped a postcard inside the book and placed it on the coffee table.

Joe leaned against the doorway from the kitchen, shaking his head. "I don't know. It all just..." He stopped and walked toward Lauren as she sobbed, sat next to her on the couch, and rested his hand on her knee. "I know. It's hard to believe."

She put her hand on top of his and looked into his eyes. "But what about the police. What did they say? They have no idea who the security guard is?"

Joe stood from the couch without an answer. He walked over to the sliding glass door and stared out across Lauren's balcony toward the parking lot below. "Nobody seems to know who he was. I'm not even sure he was a real security guard." He turned to her. "The manager at the apartment said they don't have a security guard."

Lauren stood up and walked toward him. "Then who was he?"

He gazed back at her without a word at first. "It's hard to say, because I never got a good look at the two men who showed up at my apartment, but I can't help but think this guy was one of them." He turned back to the balcony and looked through the glass. "Same size. Same build."

They both stayed quiet. Lauren stepped closer and put her hand on his arm. "So you think this all has to do with Matt Doyle?"

He glanced at her over his shoulder but again didn't answer. He didn't have any answers. But Lauren kept asking.

"Did you tell them about Matt Doyle?"

This time Joe turned to face her. "Tell who?"

"The cops?"

He huffed and let his aggravation slip through his voice. "Tell them *what*? That I'm working for a bookie I'm sure they already have on their radar?

Tell them I was there trying to find the guy who stiffed Dickie ninety grand?"

They locked gazes, and Lauren's eyes again filled with tears.

He closed his and held still. "I'm sorry, Lauren."

Her voice was soft and cracked when she spoke. "I'm just trying to help, Joe." She turned and walked back to the couch. She sat on the edge with her legs together, leaned forward with her elbows on her knees, her hands folded together. She looked toward the floor.

Joe followed her over and sat next to her. He put his arm around her. "I'm sorry."

She turned her head and looked up at him.

Joe lifted a strand of hair from her face, pushed it back on her head. He slid his hand onto her shoulder and stared into her eyes.

Neither said a word.

Lauren straightened herself up and turned to him, reached her arms out and wrapped them around his neck. She kissed him once. Then again, then pulled back and looked him in the eye.

He leaned forward into her, and she shifted her legs. She was under him and they kissed again. And this time didn't stop.

Joe's phone rang from the other room, and he sat up in the bed and looked around the bedroom. It was dark outside. He looked at the empty spot next to him in the bed, then shifted his eyes to the light coming from under the bathroom door just a few feet away.

He pulled the blanket from the bed to cover himself and hurried into the other room. He picked up his pants from the floor next to the couch and reached into his pocket for his phone. He answered, "Dickie?"

"Joey, hey, I, uh… I just heard what happened to Willie. I… I don't know what to say. I'm sorry. I'm sorry about everything."

Joe held the phone up to his ear with his shoulder, slid his jeans on with both hands and didn't respond right away.

Dickie said, "What the hell was he doing there, gettin' himself in trouble like that?"

Joe hesitated before he answered, peeked in through the bedroom doorway toward the empty bed. "Well, you want the truth? Will was helping me find Matt Doyle. You weren't very clear if you wanted me to keep doing what we'd agreed to."

"Yeah, yeah. Of course I wanted you to…" Dickie paused. "But, with what happened with Will, maybe it's not the best idea you keep—"

"I'm going to get Doyle for you, Dickie. Bring him to your door. For one thing, I need that money we agreed to. But now I need to know who did this to Will. And if Matt Doyle had something to do with it, then…"

The phone went quiet.

Lauren walked out of the bedroom, leaned toward Joe and kissed him on the cheek.

He gave her a nod and half a smile, not exactly sure how he was supposed to act after sleeping with a woman he'd been nothing more than friends with for almost twenty years. He watched her sit on the couch and put her legs up on the coffee table.

"Dickie, uh, listen… maybe we should meet. I mean, I'd like to clear the air. We've known each other for a long time, too long to let a woman come between us." He watched Lauren get up from the couch and give him a look as she walked by and headed into the kitchen.

Dickie said, "I love her, you know. I just want to make sure you understand that. And whatever happened between you two is—"

"Nothing happened, Dickie. You need to believe me." Joe pulled his watch from his pants pocket and slipped it on his wrist. He looked at the time. He'd dozed off for a bit in Lauren's bed, but it wasn't as late as he thought it was. He said into the phone, "Can you meet?" He looked through the doorway at Lauren. The smile she had on her face dropped when she turned to him.

Dickie said, "You eat?"

Joe shook his head with the phone against his ear. "Dinner? No, not yet." His eyes were still on Lauren, dressed in a pair of gym shorts and a tank top. She looked sexy, he thought.

She put a couple of glasses on the counter and

filled them with ice, pulled out a bottle of Grey Goose. She turned to him and over her shoulder said, "I don't have cranberry juice. Is OJ okay?"

"Who's that?" Dickie said.

"What? Oh... uh..." He didn't want to say, knowing he'd have to go into all the details with Dickie when he saw him. Joe could hear the clinking of glasses in the background on the other end of the phone. "Where are you?" he said.

"At Mickey Cho's. You wanna meet me here? I'll wait for you."

"Yeah, I'll meet you there. Give me a little bit, maybe half an hour or so." He hung up and saw the look on Lauren's face.

"You're leaving?" she said, holding a glass of vodka and OJ in each hand.

He held up his phone and pointed to it. "I was going to see if you wanted to come, but I need to have a man-to-man with Dickie."

"A 'man-to-man'?"

Joe hoped she'd understand. "I don't know who we're dealing with here. Clearly there's more to this guy Matt Doyle than Dickie's let on so far. And I need to make sure he's on my side."

"Why wouldn't he be on your side?"

Joe shrugged. "This girlfriend of his..."

Lauren kept her gaze on him until she turned and walked toward the refrigerator. She leaned over with the door open and looked inside. "I thought we'd grab something to eat. But I guess I'll have to eat

132

leftovers."

Joe stared at her from the doorway. "Oh, come on. You're just trying to make me feel bad."

She closed the refrigerator door and leaned back against it and looked at the floor. "No, I understand. I do. But…" She looked up at Joe and gave him a smile. "It was nice, Joe. I just hope it's not a one-night thing."

20

THE DINING ROOM and most of the tables were full at Mickey Cho's, but just a couple of people sat at the bar, at the far end, opposite from where Dickie sat.

The bartender put a plate in front of Dickie and looked at Joe. Dickie turned and, with a nod to Joe, swiveled the stool next to him. "Hey, Joey. Have a seat." He gave the bartender a nod. "Get my friend a drink, will you?"

Joe sat on the stool. "I'll have a vodka cranberry."

The bartender walked away, and Dickie slid the plate of shrimp between them.

Joe felt uncomfortable, the way everything had gone with Dickie. His eyes went to the shrimp, then he looked down the other end of the bar at the man and woman, huddled up together with martini glasses in front of them. "Listen, Dickie, I—"

"No," Dickie said. "You listen. I'm sorry. I don't

know what happened between you and Scarlett. But I think I should just—"

"Nothing happened, Dickie. That's the truth. I don't know why she told you that." He knew he'd just lied. Although *he* didn't do anything wrong. And he wasn't sure it was worth going into it. Not right then. And he wasn't prepared to go into much about her being with Matt Doyle behind Dickie's back. Mainly because he had no proof.

Dickie sipped from a martini glass. He grabbed a shrimp, dipped it in the sauce and slipped it in his mouth. He pulled the shell off the tail and tossed it in the small glass bowl, nodding toward the plate. "Go ahead, have some shrimp."

"When we were there—me and Will—we were looking for Matt Doyle. Like I told you on the phone. And I saw him outside at the pool."

"When Will was shot?"

Joe nodded. "At the Mayan Tower Apartments."

"And this was, where, in South Miami? That right?"

The bartender placed the vodka cranberry in front of Joe. Joe took a sip. He rested his elbows up on the bar and stared straight ahead with the glass in his hand. "This man walked up to Will and tried to take his camera. He was dressed like a security guard of some sort. I assumed that's what he was. But we got into it a little when I tried to help Will. Then we spotted Doyle, lounging by the pool. I knocked this guy down and ran after Doyle. But he must've known who I was. Or knew someone was looking for him, because he took off. Ran the other way and I couldn't catch him. I was a couple of blocks from the apartments when I heard the shot." Joe gave Dickie a quick glance and took another sip of his drink.

"I'm sorry about Will, Joey. I really am." He rubbed his chin. "You think this security guard shot him?"

"I don't know. I thought the guy'd come after me when I ran after Doyle. But I looked over my shoulder and he was gone."

"And nobody saw anything?"

"Nobody would talk." Joe stared straight ahead. "I got to Will, saw what'd happened to him. A woman was helping him. I didn't know it at the time, but I guess she was a nurse. She's the one told me he was dead."

Dickie leaned back in his chair, shaking his head. "I'm sorry this happened. I wish I could—"

"I just want to be clear, Dickie, that we're still in this together?"

Dickie scrunched up his face, a slight look of confusion.

Joe said, "What I mean is, are you still going to pay me to catch Matt Doyle? Because I have no doubt he had something to do with this. Maybe that guy was his bodyguard, or—"

"You sure it wasn't just a coincidence?" Dickie swiveled his stool to face Joe, one elbow rested on the back of his seat, the other on the bar. "Maybe you and Will… Maybe it was just the wrong place at the wrong time. You know what I'm saying?"

Joe sipped his drink. "Well, not that I don't need to make money. But it's personal for me now. I'm going to find him whether you want me to or not."

Dickie turned and picked up his martini. He took a sip, put it back on the bar but didn't say a word.

Joe said, "How much did Will owe you?"

Dickie's lazy eyes sprung open wide. "You think I killed him? Because he owed me a few bills?"

"No, Dickie. If I did, I would've come right out and asked you. But I'd like to know what the situation was between you and Will."

Dickie shrugged and shook his head. "I hadn't given him any action in, I don't know, maybe three years. He was what some of us considered a deadbeat. Everyone knew he was tapped out."

"Looks like I was the last to find out," Joe said.

Dickie picked up another shrimp and stuck the whole thing in his mouth, pulled the tail away and dropped it in the bowl. He wiped his mouth with the cloth napkin from his lap. "He had gambling debts, this guy I know. A small-timer, new to the game. More willing to take a risk. But as far as I know, Will was trying to pay it off, a little at a time. He slept in his office, in Miami Lakes."

Joe said, "How'd you know that?"

Dickie didn't answer, pushed the plate of shrimp closer to Joe. "Come on, I ordered enough for both of us."

Joe finally gave in, took a shrimp and dipped it in the cocktail sauce. He took half a bite, then rested what was left on his cocktail napkin. "What else do you know about Matt Doyle? This friend of his, owns the apartments where he stayed... name is Idél Del Rio."

Dickie stared back at Joe. "Idél?" He shook his head. "Never heard of him. But I remember at one point, not too long ago, there was this big guy tried to get in on some action. He was a beard for Doyle."

"A beard?"

"Yeah. A beard. You know, guy who'll place a bet for you when you get cut off, like Doyle did. Guy meets me, wants to put down a big dime. I got the feeling it was a bailout. So I sniffed him out, just the stupid bets he wanted to make, reminded me of Doyle. I asked him if he knew him."

"If he knew Matt Doyle?"

Dickie said, "I asked him, the guy got up and walked out. Didn't say another word." He leaned toward Joe, lowered his voice. "Losers like Doyle, they all think the same way. You can sniff out the mush artists pretty fast when you've been in the business as long as I have."

Joe thought about it and wanted to tell him what he thought about Scarlett. Maybe go right ahead, tell him she came on to him at his apartment, shoved her tongue straight down his throat. Tell him how he pushed her off of him but leave out the part it took him a few seconds to do it.

"I'm going to get Doyle for you, Dickie. But you have to promise you'll let me do what I have to do."

Dickie shrugged. "What's that supposed to mean?"

Joe hesitated. "I know you don't think Scarlett knows anything about him, or where he might be hiding, but…"

"You want to talk to her? See if she'll help?"

Joe shook his head. "I don't know if that'll do me any good." He sipped his drink and gathered his thoughts before he continued. "I'd like to keep an eye on her. Maybe see where she goes when you're not around."

Dickie stared back at Joe and narrowed his eyes a bit. "I don't know. I trust Scarlett, Joey. I mean, I'm not a fool. Of course she's got her secrets and maybe a past she doesn't want me to know about, but…"

"She won't know a thing. And I'll make sure she's safe. I just… there's no denying she knows Matt Doyle."

Dickie was quiet for a couple of moments. "What if I talk to her? Have a heart-to-heart; give her a chance to be straight with me?"

"No!" Joe said. "Please, I'm asking you to trust me on this. Let's just keep things quiet. And hopefully I'm wrong; she has nothing at all to do with Doyle. And you two can go on, live happily ever after."

21

JOE ADJUSTED THE Glock in his pants and walked toward the entrance to Will's office building. He pulled open the glass door and took a quick look behind him. He wasn't exactly paranoid but wondered if someone had, by some chance, followed him.

He took the stairs and walked down the hall toward Will's office. Will had left his keys in Joe's car, but Joe had no idea which one would fit the lock on the door. He tried four of them before one finally slid inside without resistance. He turned the knob and stood in the doorway after he pushed open the door. He stared at Will's empty desk.

Joe didn't know exactly why he was there or what he was looking for. The truth was when you gambled and didn't pay your debts, at some point you were going to end up with a target on your back.

He stepped inside and looked around the small office and the old wooden paneling on the walls, like it was 1978. His eyes went to the white pillow on top of the blankets folded in the corner. A framed, black-and-white photo on the wall caught his eye. He remembered when Will took it. Made the front page, along with Joe's article, after mob boss Victor "9-Iron" Merloni was arrested outside one of his nightclubs in South Beach.

He looked behind the open door, spotted a wooden baseball bat leaned up against the edge of the casing. He picked up the bat and looked at the barrel, signed by Andre "The Hawk" Dawson when he was with the Marlins.

Will didn't have many friends. He used to talk about it like he was bragging. He said he didn't need them and didn't have a problem being alone. He was the type of guy who'd go to the movies alone. Go on vacation alone. Joe couldn't remember him ever having a woman in his life. Other than one he'd pay for.

He walked around to the other side of Will's desk, rolled the chair back and sat. He turned in the chair and leaned the bat against the wall behind him, turned back to the desk and opened one of the lower drawers. He pulled out a bottle of Wild Turkey, almost empty, and placed it up on top of the desk. He reached back inside the drawer and pulled out a bottle of pills. He looked at the label, but it was blank. He removed the cap and dumped the pills in the palm of his hand, held it close to his face and examined each one. The pills were engraved with a V. All he could guess was it was a bottle of Vicodin, but he knew the way the marketing people came up with names for prescription drugs: it could've been anything.

But maybe his friend had just fallen a lot harder than he'd let on.

Joe had his eyes in the drawer, moved around the staples, pens, and pads of Post-it Notes stuffed inside. He heard a click and looked up.

The security guard from the apartment, or whatever he was, still in his generic uniform, had a gun pointed at Joe.

Joe looked past the man at a Latino still out in the hall, short and stocky with a clean, bald head and a thick patch of bleach-blond hair on his chin. Joe stood from the desk with his hands up so they could see he wasn't armed. Or to see he at least wasn't holding a gun.

"Now that I see you together, I guess we don't need to introduce ourselves." His eyes shifted to the shorter one. "I believe you and your friend were at my apartment?"

Neither one of them answered Joe.

The short one brushed past his friend. "You got a gun in those pants? Put it up on the desk, or my friend will take it out for you." He had a slight accent, almost sounded like he said "Ju" instead of "You." But otherwise, clear English.

Joe lifted his shirt, pulled his Glock from his waistband and placed it on the desk in front of him. He didn't need any trouble. He looked past them both and out into the hallway. The place was empty. He'd only been to Will's office a handful of times but never saw anyone else. He wondered how the landlord made any money.

He nodded toward the short, stocky one. "You must be Idél?"

The man stared back at him before he answered, then gave Joe a slight nod. "I am."

He looked from the tall guy to Idél. "Which one of you did it?"

"Did *what?*" Idél said.

Joe looked him in the eye. "Killed my friend."

Idél shook his head. "I wasn't there, my friend." He pointed with his thumb to the big man. "And this one was chasing you on Fifty-Ninth. No?"

The two exchanged another look and the tall one nodded, still hadn't said a word. He wiggled the muzzle of his gun toward Joe. "Let's go."

Joe shifted his eyes between the two, then shook his head. "I'm not going anywhere."

Idél looked up at his friend and laughed, then turned and looked out into the hall. He turned back with a nod toward Joe. "I don't think we're giving you a choice, my friend."

The taller one reached over the desk and tried to grab Joe's arm.

But Joe stood up from the chair and slapped the

man's hand away. "You're going to have to shoot me, you want me to go with you."

Idél smiled and shrugged. "If you insist."

Joe kept his eyes on the tall one with the gun. "Why don't you just tell me what the hell's going on here."

"Why don't *you* tell *me* what's going on," Idél said. "Why are you after Mr. Doyle?"

Joe said, "I don't think that's any of your business."

Idél gave the big man a quick nod, and the man took one long step around the side of the desk, swung the pistol in his hand and hit Joe in the mouth.

Joe's head jerked around. He felt like he'd been whacked with a club. Blood dripped from the corner of his mouth and down his chin. But he didn't put his hand to his face or show any sign of pain. Even though there was plenty of it. He stared back at Idél. "He owes someone some money. It's a significant amount."

Idél stared back at him. "Significant? Like how much?"

"Ninety grand."

Idél laughed. "Maybe that is a lot to a writer, like yourself, but…"

Before Idél could finish, Joe reached back for the bat he'd leaned against the wall behind him. He came up with a good long swing and struck the tall one in the hand.

The gun fell to the floor, and the man screamed, squeezing his bloody hand.

Idél reached into his pants and came out with a pistol of his own, but Joe already had the Glock on him, the bat in his other hand. "Put it down."

Idél eased the gun by his side, and the big guy reached down to pick up his.

But Joe came down with the bat and struck the man on the back of the head, sent him crashing to the floor. When the man tried to get up, Joe said, "Stay there, unless you want a bullet in the back of your head.

The man didn't listen and reached for his gun, but Joe didn't want to take the Glock off Idél, so he took another swing and hit the man's arm. He felt the crack.

"My arm!" the man yelled. "You broke my arm."

Idél backed away from the doorway and into the hall, his gun still in his hand but by his side.

"Get the hell out of here," Joe said. His voice was calm, but he could feel his heart pounding in his chest. His ears were ringing. He kept the gun pointed through the doorway on Idél, then used the end of the bat and prodded the big man down on the floor on all fours. "You hear me, Lurch? Get the hell out of here."

The big man got up and ran, stumbled into the open door and made it out of the office without looking back.

They both hurried down the hall and left through

the door to the stairwell.

Joe fell back into the chair and let out the breath he held. He leaned over and picked up the gun from the floor. He looked it over and placed it on the desk in front of him.

He had no doubt Idél and the goon were still around, maybe even waiting for him outside. He knew he had to call someone, get some help. He stuck the big man's gun in the lower drawer and stood up, tucked the Glock in his pants and walked into the hall. He couldn't believe how empty the place was. Not a soul in sight.

He pulled the door closed behind him and headed for the stairs but kept the Glock out in front of him. He was careful with each step and tried not to make any noise.

At the bottom of the stairs he lifted his foot and kicked open the heavy steel door with the illuminated EXIT sign above it. He stepped outside into the bright sunlight with his gun drawn. The smell of burning rubber smacked him in the nose. He looked toward the parking lot and saw the flames coming from the Mercedes. Fire and black smoke poured out the windows from inside.

"Son of a bitch," he said. He tucked the Glock in his pants and started for the lot. And within that split second he let down his guard, something hard struck the top of his head. He dropped to his knees and was hit again, this time against his neck. He felt a tingle in his feet and saw the concrete beneath him as his body collapsed to the ground.

22

JOE OPENED HIS eyes and tried to sit up, but the man kneeling over him held him down with a hand on his chest. "Take it easy, sir. You're all right; you just need to relax." Joe leaned back and looked up at what he realized was a paramedic. His eyes shifted to another man standing behind the paramedic.

"Bart?" he said. "What are you doing here?" He pushed himself up and looked past the two men leaning over him. The Mercedes was still there, but three quarters of it blackened from the fire. The trunk was the only part of the car that was still yellow. Firefighters sprayed water on it as it smoldered. A toxic smell filled the air and gave Joe a sick feeling.

Bart was dressed in his brown Miami-Dade Police Department uniform. Or his Metro uniform, as some still called it. "I was just going to ask you the same thing," he said.

Joe gave him a confused look.

Bart said, "What are *you* doing out here, Joe?"

The paramedic held a towel against the back of Joe's head.

Joe pushed him away. "I'm fine. Really." He looked toward the car.

The paramedic handed Joe the towel. "You gotta keep pressure on it. Got a pretty good cut back there."

Joe grabbed the towel and pushed himself up to his feet. "Was I knocked out?" He stumbled a bit when he took a step.

His friend Bart reached out to help him. "Out cold."

Joe pulled his arm from Bart's grasp. "I'm okay." He glanced at the steel door on the building he remembered stepping out of before he was struck on the head. He reached for his waist hoping he had his Glock. He looked around the ground but didn't see it. And he didn't say anything to Bart about it.

Bart nodded toward another officer walking toward them. He waved him off. "He's all right. I'll take care of it." He grabbed Joe by the arm, and this time Joe didn't resist. They walked toward the green-and-white Miami-Dade cruiser. "Maybe you should have a seat," Bart said. "You don't look so good." He glanced at the yellow and charcoal-black Mercedes. "That your car?"

Joe had the bloodstained towel up against the back of his head. "It was. It belongs to a friend."

Bart looked him in the eye and paused a moment. "Dickie Caldwell?"

Joe didn't answer.

Bart said, "Thought so." He shifted his stance. "What about the Mossberg in the trunk?"

"What about it? It's legal."

"I didn't say it wasn't. Just surprised to see it in there, that's all."

Joe pulled the towel from the back of his head, looked at the bloodstain, and put it back. "As you can see, I'm in a little bit of trouble."

The paramedic crouched and gathered his things from the ground. He looked up at Joe, then over to Bart. "He could use a stitch or two, you know."

"It won't heal without?" Joe said.

The paramedic started past him with his medical box in his hand. "Even if you're not going to let us take you, I still recommend you go to the ER. But, yes, you'll probably be okay if you don't mind a big scar on the back of your head."

Bart shrugged and gave the paramedic a nod. "He's got plenty of hair on that thick head of his." He watched the paramedic step into the driver's side of the EMT vehicle, then turned back to Joe. "So what're you doing with Dickie Caldwell's car with a shotgun in the back?" He put his hands on his hips. "And who the hell did this to you?"

Joe didn't answer, walked across the lot toward the Mercedes. Or at least what was left of it. He looked over his shoulder and said to Bart, "Dickie still runs Ray's Auto Repair, hooked me up with the old Mercedes when—"

"Runs it?" Bart laughed. "Dickie doesn't know his ass from a fuel pump. And you know it." He caught up with Joe and stood next to him, both their eyes on the car. "There's only one reason Dickie owns that place."

Joe looked at the towel again and showed the bloodstain to Bart. "See, the bleeding already stopped." He looked back toward the building. "You still didn't tell me what you're doing out this way."

"You haven't told me either." They both exchanged a look. Bart said, "I wanted to retire, get a cushy job somewhere watching the door. But they convinced me to stay on for another year, then transferred me to the Northwest Division."

"Retire, huh?" Joe thought about it. He always pictured himself retiring from the *Post*, the ceremonious departure, the gold watch. No such luck.

"Been thirty-two years," Bart said. "But with the shortage… kids don't want to be police officers anymore. At least not the ones on the street." He shrugged and glanced around the parking lot. "Can you blame them?" He turned and walked toward his cruiser. He opened the door. "You need a ride somewhere? Maybe to the ER, get that crack in your head checked?" He reached toward the front seat, came out with a clipboard, slammed the door closed, and walked back toward Joe. "I don't know how much you can tell me, or how much you want to tell me. But I can't leave here without some kind of statement."

Joe shrugged. "I came out of the building and got jumped. Could've just been a couple of kids, whacked me on the back of the head." He stared back at Bart, liked he'd expected him to call his bluff.

"Oh, so what you're telling me is some kids lit your car on fire, whacked you on the head with a blunt object, for shits and giggles?"

Joe looked away.

Bart said, "This have anything to do with Will?"

"I wasn't sure you'd heard."

Bart nodded. "Of course I heard. I'm a cop. But I didn't know you were there with him until this morning. South Miami's handling it, so I don't have the whole story. But I know he had his private investigator's license, although he hadn't renewed it."

"You sure?" Joe said.

Bart let out a slight laugh. "I could see you doing something like that. But Will?" He shook his head. "No wonder he got—" He stopped mid-sentence. "I'm sorry, Joe. I didn't mean to…"

"It's all right. Will had his problems." Joe looked down. "But he was actually helping me. That's why he was there. So I'm feeling a bit responsible for what happened."

"You going to tell me what you were doing there?"

Joe looked Bart in the eye and shook his head. "I think it'll be best for both of us I don't. Not now."

Bart rolled his eyes. "Joe, how long've we known each other? Have I ever gotten in your way? I know you newspaper guys working the crime scene. You all wanna be cops deep inside." He let out a slight laugh.

Joe reached up and touched his ear, then winced in pain. "Son of a bitch. That hurts."

"Your ear?"

Joe nodded. "I thought so. I got hit more than once."

"You're a big guy, Joe. If someone's going to take you down, I'd hope they're smart enough to swing twice." He turned and looked toward the upper levels of the building. "So why don't you at least tell me what you were doing here." He looked back at the yellow Jeep. "That belongs to Will, huh?"

"Yeah, why? You run the plate?"

"It was the only other vehicle in the lot when we got here."

Joe stared at Will's Jeep. "Will had an office upstairs. But, to be honest, I've never seen anyone else in the place. The lot's always empty like this."

They both turned to look when a flatbed truck pulled into the parking lot and backed up in front of the Mercedes. The driver got out and gave them a quick nod, then got down on the asphalt with a chain in his hand.

Bart yelled, "Still hot under there." The man gave him a glance but crawled on his back under the front of the car, hooked the chain up somewhere underneath.

Bart looked at the clipboard in his hand, held it up toward Joe. "I gotta put something down. Can't just say you just happened to be in the area." He stared back at Joe, then stepped over to the cruiser and pulled open the driver's side door. He tossed the clipboard inside. "We can do it later." He slammed the door and folded his arms. "So why don't you tell me what's going on. Off the record."

Joe huffed out a slight laugh. "You sound like a reporter." He watched the truck driver crank the chain and pull what was left of the Mercedes up onto the flatbed. There was no rubber on the front wheels and they scraped going up the steel ramp. "Where's the Mossberg?"

"I got it." Bart walked around the back of the cruiser and popped open the lid on the trunk. "I'm the only one who saw it, so…"

"It's legal."

Bart reached in for the Mossberg, looked it over. "I like these Mossbergs." His eyes went to Joe. "You shoot it?"

Joe shook his head. "No. Not yet."

23

LAUREN WALKED FROM the kitchen with a towel and a clear plastic bag of ice. She handed it to Joe and stood in front of him next to the coffee table.

Joe moved over on the couch. "You want to sit?"

She shook her head. "Keep the ice on it, will you?"

Joe wrapped the towel around the bag and held it up against the back of his head. "You all right?" he said. "You have that look on your face."

She turned from him, went over and sat in the only other chair in the room in the corner, next to the TV across from Joe. "Well, this whole thing with Will has me a little concerned." She shrugged. "You didn't make it sound like this would be dangerous work."

Joe tried to force a smile. "It's not. At least, not for *you*. You're the behind-the-scenes person. Isn't that how you like it?"

"I need to find something, Joe."

"Find something?"

"A job. The severance doesn't add up."

"When I find Doyle, Dickie's going to pay me. And I'm going to need your help, Lauren. You know I'm not greedy. We'll get more from this one job than you'll get in six months going back to—"

"I don't know if I can do it, Joe. I'm scared. I'm scared for you. The whole thing is just…" She paused. "What are you going to do? Be some kind of vigilante?"

"They killed my friend, Lauren. *Our* friend."

"I know that. It's just…" She again shifted her eyes to Joe. "What about your writing? The world still needs good writers."

"What's that got to do with me?" he said.

"You are one of the best. You know that."

"The days are gone someone's going to pay three grand for a column. Not when they can get some kid who doesn't even live in the States to write it for forty bucks."

"Not the kind of writing you're capable of, Joe."

He leaned back on the couch, held the towel with the ice down on his lap. "You were smart to get into social media, doing the research, the quick snippets. That's all people read today. All people do is skim the headlines." He looked her in the eye, shook his head and winced. He reached up and felt behind his ear. "Shit, this hurts."

Lauren got up from her chair and walked down the hall, came back with a small red box in her hand. "I still read," she said. "I read a lot. And so do most of the people I know." She placed the red box on the coffee table, sat next to Joe on the couch and opened a small bottle of rubbing alcohol. "Turn around," she said, then slid closer to him, soaked a gauze pad with alcohol and dabbed it on the back of Joe's head.

"People *our* age might read, but…"

"What are you going to do? Be Dickie's new goon? Get your head knocked all over the place?"

"I didn't say that's what I wanted to do. But"—he turned and looked back at her over his shoulder—"when I was younger, I thought I'd end up in law enforcement. A cop or the FBI, or…"

"It's a little late for that, don't you think?"

Joe shrugged. "Will was doing it. I mean, as a private investigator."

"He was broke, wasn't he?" She dabbed the wound on his head with the cotton ball, then squeezed ointment onto a gauze pad and rubbed it on his head. "This is worse than I thought," she said. "You probably could've used stitches. But it's too late at this point. It's already started to heal."

Joe turned to her when she was done. "I still need your help. And without Will around, well…"

"I told you I'll do what I can. But I'm not interested in dying. Not yet, anyway."

Lauren gave Joe a ride back to his place and went inside with him, brought her computer and had it out in front of her when she looked up, watched him at the turntable, turning over an album.

He flipped Bob Dylan's *Blood on the Tracks* over to side two, moved the needle to the fourth track, "Shelter from the Storm." He stood still, watched the album turn. He gave Lauren a look, then walked down the end of the shelves, lifted the framed Barbara Streisand poster. "Did I show you this? Picked it up when I went to see Juan."

"I didn't know you were a fan."

"A fan?" He shrugged. "I like Barbara Streisand. But I thought it was cool." He gave the framed poster another look, then leaned it back against the wall.

Lauren leaned back on the kitchen chair and pointed to her laptop. "Maybe you should talk to Bart. This guy Idél Del Rio's got a record, looks like he spent a few years behind bars."

He walked toward the kitchen and looked over Lauren's shoulder. "What'd he do?"

"Kidnapping."

Joe leaned on the back of her chair and stared at the screen. "How long was he in?"

"He did three of a five-year sentence. Got out two years ago, up in Baker."

Joe straightened up and thought for a moment. "I wonder how long he's owned those apartments?"

Lauren didn't answer but clicked the trackpad on her laptop and brought up another page. "See this guy?"

Joe nodded. "That's him. The big guy from outside the apartment when Will was shot. He was at my office with Idél."

"He was a guard at Baker Correctional. His name's Eugene Melrose."

Joe leaned on her chair again and looked over her shoulder. "Anything else about him?"

She glanced at Joe. "He was fired from Baker for looking the other way when a prisoner allegedly hung himself."

"Allegedly?"

"He said he was asleep, missed the call check. That's when the inmate hung himself with a bedsheet."

Joe stared at the image of Eugene Melrose, pictured him grabbing Will's camera, then standing there in front of him in Will's office before Joe whacked him with the bat. "What about Matt Doyle? How are these three connected?"

She shook her head. "I'm not sure yet. Neither are anywhere on any social channels, other than the connections we already made to Scarlett's sister and Matt's cousin."

Joe walked into the other room and stood by his turntable. "I'm sure Doyle won't be back at those apartments anytime soon. Not now that he knows we're looking for him."

She stood up from the chair and walked toward Joe. "Don't you think it's more important you find Idél and Eugene? I mean, I know you want to do the work Dickie asked you to do, but…"

"What's wrong with getting all three? I get Doyle; it puts money in my pocket. I get Idél and Eugene… I get revenge."

24

JOE HAD GONE back to Will's office and got his Jeep, still parked outside in the lot where he last saw it. He wondered if the repo man would show up to take it. But no harm driving it for as long as he could. Especially since he had no other wheels.

He pulled into Dickie's driveway, and Scarlett was outside with her back to him, a hose in her hand spraying the flower garden by the garage.

Joe lifted his phone and took a picture of Scarlett before she noticed he was there, then stepped out from the Jeep.

She turned with a pleasant look on her face but kept the water going. She didn't say a word, then turned back to the flowers.

Joe wondered what was going through that mind of hers. He walked up to her wearing his sunglasses. She was an attractive woman, no doubt. But crazy as they came.

She turned and looked at him over her shoulder. "Dickie's not here." Her eyes went to the Jeep. "Where's the Mercedes?"

He couldn't help but think she already knew exactly what had happened to it. He almost told her he traded it for the Jeep to see her reaction. But he didn't have time to mess around and wanted to do what he could to get her on his good side. "Dickie loves you, you know."

She let go of the nozzle and dropped the hose at her feet. She cracked a slight smile. "That's what he tells me."

"Well, I'd like to know why you'd tell him I came on to you. When we both know what happened."

She gave Joe a look similar to one she'd given him when she was at his place. "I didn't know he'd react the way he did. I wasn't lying when I said he was okay with me hanging around other guys, but—"

"What would make you think he'd be cool with that? Of course he'd tell you it didn't bother him. He doesn't want you to feel he'd hold you back from doing whatever you want. That's how Dickie is." Joe lifted his sunglasses from his eyes and placed them on his head. "But you still lied to him. Because what you told him never happened. I never came on to you, Scarlett. And you know it."

She turned from him and crouched in front of the flower bed, pulled a pair of small clippers from her back pocket and deadheaded the blooming lantana. Still with her back to him, she said, "I think it's water under the bridge now, isn't it?" She gave him a quick glance over her shoulder. "Didn't you meet him at Mickey Cho's?"

Joe stared at her from behind. "He told you?"

She glanced back at him again over her shoulder. "Dickie tells me everything." She kept her gaze on him.

Joe didn't like the look at all. He hesitated for a few seconds. "Why are you with him?"

She stood up and with a slight tilt to her head, said, "*Why am I with him?* What kind of question is that?"

"Let me ask another way. Can you look me in the eye, tell me you feel the same way about him as he does about you?"

She didn't hesitate. "Of course I do. I love Dickie. What's not to love?" She didn't take her eyes off Joe.

"If that's true, then I hope you won't do anything to hurt him."

She winked back at Joe with a smile, her nose crinkled. "Oh, isn't that cute? You're threatening me? Just to protect your friend." She looked at Joe. "Dickie doesn't need you to protect him."

The smile was off her face.

Joe looked at her hand. The diamond ring she'd worn when he first met her was gone. "Where's the diamond ring?"

She followed Joe's eyes to her fingers. "A diamond ring?"

Joe nodded. "The one you stole from Daniel Doyle's wife. I know that was you. *Pam*."

Scarlett's mouth hung open. She was quiet for a moment, then swallowed. "Pam?"

"Isn't that the name you used when you were there with Matt?" Joe said.

Scarlett turned from him, crouched down and started working in the flowers again. "I have no idea what you're talking about. I have nothing to do with Matt Doyle anymore. He wasn't even my boyfriend, like you may think. We fooled around once or twice, but…"

"Then why were you at the Mayan Tower Apartments? Where he was staying?"

Scarlett was still crouched down. She finally stood up and gazed back at him. "I don't know anything about the Mayan Towers, or whatever you just said. I've never even heard of it. So, I don't know who told you I was there, but…" She narrowed her eyes. "You know what? Whatever I do is none of your goddamn business. That goes for my relationship with Dickie. I think it's time you stay out of our business." She tossed the clippers in the soil around the flower bed and walked away, toward the steps at the front of Dickie's house. She pulled open the front door and disappeared inside without another word.

Joe drove out to Daniel Doyle's condo with the

picture he took of Scarlett. It wasn't a perfect shot —a side profile—but enough to see if Daniel Doyle would know if she was the woman there with his cousin, Matt. And enough to know if she was the woman Matt called "Pam," and who stole Daniel's wife's—actually his *ex*-wife's—ring.

He wasn't exactly sure what he was out to do. He wanted to find Matt Doyle and collect what he had coming. He wanted to prove to Dickie that Scarlett was no good, that she was still with Matt Doyle. And that she's likely somewhat connected to whoever killed Will.

He stepped off the elevator down the hall from Daniel Doyle's apartment. He could see Daniel's door was slightly ajar.

He stood in front of it and tried to look in through the crack but decided to knock before he'd walk in. The door opened another few inches when his knuckles hit the wood. He stepped closer and again tried to look inside. He sniffed when an odor hit him in the nose. All he could think of was burnt toast.

He pushed the door open and stepped inside. "Daniel? It's Joe Sheldon." He took a few more steps. "Hello?" Joe wished he'd replaced the Glock he assumed Idél and Eugene had taken when they knocked him out, outside Will's office. He looked around for something to grab but continued toward an open doorway.

The burnt smell grew stronger with each step. He

walked into a kitchen filled with smoke and called out again. "Daniel?" And as soon as he said his name, the smoke alarm went off above him. Through the smoke he saw the toaster there on the counter. Smoke poured from the top. He reached for the plug and pulled it from the wall, then grabbed a cloth from the handle on the stove and waved it in the air under the screaming smoke detector.

He continued through the kitchen and down a hall. He saw an open door.

And there was Daniel, his head on the desk with his face turned to the side, resting on disheveled papers covered in blood.

Joe took a step closer, leaned over and got a look at Daniel's face with his vacant eyes staring, the tan color of his skin replaced with a bluish purple.

Without question, Daniel Doyle was dead.

25

JOE'S PHONE RANG. He leaned toward the front of his couch and placed his vodka cranberry on the coffee table. He reached for his phone and saw it was Bart.

Joe tapped the screen to answer and put the phone up to his ear. "Bart?"

"Joe? Where the hell are you?"

"Where am I? At my apartment, getting drunk."

"Why didn't you call me?"

"I don't know. I was planning on it. The neighbor's with the Miami-Dade PD, showed up a minute after I hung up with nine-one-one."

"I know that. He's the one who called me, said you mentioned my name."

Joe reached for his glass and sipped his drink, leaned back on the couch. "Hope that's all right."

"Of course it is. I just wish you'd called me yourself. I could've at least gotten involved a little sooner. But now…"

The line went quiet.

"But now *what*? I took off out of there after I answered whatever questions I could."

"Nobody's contacted you?"

Joe hesitated, shrugged a shoulder as if Bart could see through the phone. "Like who?"

"*Like who?* From the Miami-Dade Police Department, that's who. After you left, someone called and said they saw you in the building earlier in the week."

Joe leaned forward on the couch and put his glass back on the table. He reached for the bottle of vodka and topped it off but didn't get up to get any cranberry. He took a sip and stood up, walked over toward the door to the balcony. "I was there asking about Matt Doyle. He's Daniel Doyle's cousin."

"Then why'd you tell the officers on the scene you didn't know him?"

"I don't know him. I didn't say I'd never talked to him before. But the way they asked their questions…" Joe stared out into the darkness outside.

Bart said, "They want to talk to you. I don't know what it means just yet, but… I'm not sure why nobody's contacted you by now. I'll have to look into it."

"Is that it?" Joe said.

Bart was silent before he answered. "He was shot with your gun, Joe."

"My gun?"

"A Glock, registered under your name."

Joe turned from the glass door. "Oh shit," he said.

"Oh shit *what?*"

"My Glock. They took it from me when I was attacked at Will's office." He sipped his drink and walked into the kitchen. He reached in the freezer and grabbed a couple of cubes, dropped them in his glass and shook it around. He poured cranberry juice over the top.

Bart said, "You had another gun? Besides the Mossberg?"

Joe didn't respond.

"Joe?" Bart paused. "You're going to need to be straight with me."

"About the gun? Yeah, Bart... of course. I just —"

"Joe, let me explain to you where we might have a slight problem here. The thing is, I didn't take a statement from you. So we don't have any documentation to back up anything about a missing gun."

"You didn't file a report?" Joe walked back toward the sliding glass door and pulled it open, walked out onto the balcony.

"I did. Just not enough to help you out of what could turn out to be a real shit show if you can't prove your Glock was stolen."

"But I called nine-one-one, Bart. Who the hell

would call nine-one-one if he killed a man."

Bart didn't answer, but Joe heard a knock at his door. He walked to the door and put his eye up against the peephole. "Shit, Bart. Got a couple of officers at my door."

"Okay, okay. Listen, don't say more than you have to. Let me see what I can do. You can go ahead and mention my name, but…"

"All right, Bart. I gotta go." He tapped the screen on his phone and let it hang by his side. He unlocked the door and pulled it open.

"Officer?" He forced a weak smile. "Is there something wrong?"

Lauren walked with Joe down the steps from the Miami-Dade pretrial detention center. She turned to him. "Why didn't you call me last night?" She unlocked the passenger side for him, then walked around to the other side and kept her eyes on him from across the roof.

"I waited to see what bail'd be set at." He pulled open the door. "How'd you get the money?"

"I called Ralph." She stepped inside and watched him as he ducked into the passenger seat. "But I'm talking about before you were arrested. Why didn't you call me back? I left you a couple of messages."

Joe hesitated before he turned to her and smiled, his lips tight together. "I know. I'm sorry. I just had to gather my thoughts." He shook his head and stared straight ahead through the windshield. "I was going to call you back. Never imagined I'd be arrested."

He watched her slide the key in the ignition, her eyebrows turned up. She had a worried look on her face. The engine started and she sat still, then turned to him. "You didn't do it, Joe. Did you?"

He cocked his head back. "Jesus Christ, Lauren. Are you serious?" He shook his head. "All I did was go to Daniel Doyle's place to show him a picture of Scarlett, see if she was the woman there with his cousin when his ex-wife's ring went missing."

She shifted the car into reverse, turned in her seat and backed out of the parking space. "Why's it matter?"

"Why's *what* matter?"

"If it was Scarlett?"

"Of course it matters. She claims she has nothing to do with Matthew Doyle. But she's lying. Her own sister followed her to the apartment building where Will was killed."

Lauren drove east on Northwest Fourteenth and took the ramp for 395. "Did you explain that to the cops?"

"About Scarlett?" He shook his head. "I told them what I thought I had to. And I'm not sure they'd believe me either way."

Lauren gave him a quick glance and took the exit for Second Avenue. "None of this is easy to follow, Joe."

"Which part?"

"Well, you started off, all you had to do was locate some deadbeat gambler."

Joe watched her and waited for more.

She gave him a glance, then shifted her eyes back to the road. "You're a writer, Joe. But you go out and buy a couple of guns. Next thing you know, some guy's dead. And the bullet that killed him belongs to one of the guns you just happen to own?"

"You think I killed him?"

She shook her head. "No. Of course not. But it's just a lot to digest. And I think, at this point, you're in over your head."

Joe stared at her from the passenger seat. "These people killed Will."

She turned up Biscayne Avenue. "So then, this is all about Will? Because you bought those guns before he—"

"Of *course* it's about Will. But it's all tied together. Don't you get that?"

She pulled up in front of his building and put the Subaru in park. She shifted in her seat to face him. "It doesn't matter if I get it or not. You're the one going to prison if the cops don't get it right. Maybe for the rest of your life."

Joe put his hand on the door's handle and looked out the window toward his building. He turned back to Lauren with a smile. "At least I'd have plenty of time to write."

Lauren stared back at him, not even a hint of a smile. "You think this is a joke? You're lucky they even let you out on bail, Joe." She put her hand on his leg. Her eyes were glossy with tears. "Aren't you scared?"

He kept his eyes on hers but took a moment before he answered. Drops of rain had started to bounce off the windshield. "I don't have time to be scared." He put his hand over hers, then leaned forward and gave her a kiss. "I'll call you later."

Joe started to pull his hand away, but she squeezed it tight. "Do you want me to come inside with you?"

He was looking out toward the building again, then back at her as he pushed open the passenger door. "I'm going to shower. Then I need to find a lawyer." He stepped out of her car, turned, then leaned his head back inside. "I'll call you later."

26

JOE BIT INTO his grilled cheese and watched Bart walk toward his booth after he went outside to take a call.

Bart slid into the booth across from Joe. "Nobody got her name." He stuck a fry in his mouth.

"One of the other people there said she was a nurse," Joe said. "Had blood on her hands, held Will's head on her lap." He shook his head. "How could she just disappear like that?"

"It happens," Bart said. "You know that, don't you? Could be scared, slipped away with all the commotion before she had to get involved."

Joe looked toward the other end of the diner. "He was shot at close range. I guess I just wonder if —"

"If she was the one who shot him?" Bart shook his head. "You think she'd stick around, try and help the guy?"

"Eugene Melrose, the fake security guard, was on Seventy-Fourth, chasing after me. If there were people around up there, near where Will was shot, who knows? Woman goes up to Will, plugs him with her pistol, lays him down and tells everyone she's a nurse." Joe held his grilled cheese in his hand but didn't take a bite. "Then she takes off soon as she has a chance."

Bart ate another fry. His eyes were up on the small TV in the corner behind the counter. "I don't know, Joe. Maybe you should've been a novelist. Write crime fiction." He huffed out a laugh. "You have an imagination, Joe. It's just a little far-fetched."

Joe stared back at Bart without a word, his eyes somewhat narrowed. "Is it?" He took another bite of his grilled cheese, then dropped what was left on his plate. "Maybe that's why you never made detective, Bart. You don't have any imagination at all."

They both locked eyes on one another.

"I'm sorry," Joe said. "I don't mean that."

Bart shifted his eyes back to the TV. "You're a goddamn writer, Joe. I don't know why the hell you think that makes you qualified to play detective." He leaned to one side and pulled his wallet from his back pocket, took out a twenty and stood up from the table. He tossed it in front of Joe.

"Bart, wait," Joe said.

Bart kept walking for the door.

"Bart? Come on, man. I need your help."

Bart stopped before he turned for the door, then slowly looked back at Joe. He walked to the table and slid back into the booth. "You've got yourself in some deep shit, Joe. You start pushing friends away who can help."

Joe had a fry in his hand but put it back on his plate. "Bart, I didn't mean what I said."

"You forget I turned down the position, Joe. If I wanted to be detective, I could've—"

"You don't need to explain. I'm an idiot. Let's just forget I said anything, okay?"

Bart leaned forward on the table. "You want to play some kind of hero?" He shook his head. "Your number one priority has to be to clear your own name. From what it sounds like to me, you're holding back some information that could help you. And if you're worried about getting Dickie in hot water, then—"

"All Dickie asked me to do was find someone. There's nothing criminal about that."

Bart stared back at Joe. "You believe what you want, Joe. But you somehow chose the wrong path for your freelance work. And look where it's gotten you."

Joe was behind the wheel of Will's Jeep when his phone rang. He pulled over into the breakdown lane on the South Dixie when he saw it was Dickie.

"Joey," he said, his voice loud and excited. "Where are you?"

Joe could hear something in his voice. "Dickie? Is everything all right?"

"It's Scarlett. She's been kidnapped. They're going to kill her if—"

"Dickie, calm down. Tell me what happened."

"I… I don't know. I got home; there was a letter stuck in the door. There was a picture of her taped to it. She was tied up."

Joe couldn't believe what he was hearing. Or maybe he did. "What's the note say?"

"It was a letter, typed. The photo's one of those old Polaroids."

"Can you read it to me?"

Dickie took a moment, then said, "Yeah. It says, *Do not call the police. Do not try to find her. If you want to see her alive again, you have twenty-four hours to pay three hundred thousand dollars in cash.*"

The line went quiet.

"Anything else?" Joe said.

Dickie sounded like he got choked up on the other end of the phone. "Joey, you gotta help me find her."

Joe said, "What about where to deliver the money? Or how to deliver it? There must be a—"

"Nothing. I read you the whole note."

Joe thought about it. "Okay, Dickie, listen. She'll be fine. Don't worry. I'll help you."

"Can you come out to the house?"

Joe looked up ahead on the highway. "Give me half an hour. Anybody calls or you hear anything else, call me right away."

27

JOE STOOD OUTSIDE Morgan's apartment, knocked and tried to listen through the door. He looked at his watch and knocked one more time. He waited another minute, then turned and headed back for the elevators.

He pressed the button and watched the lights above the door as the elevator climbed from the lower floors until it dinged. The elevator door slid open.

Morgan stepped off and into the hallway with her grocery bags in each arm.

It took Joe a few seconds to recognize her, with a baseball cap pulled low and a pair of tight shorts. She started past him, then stopped and looked right at him. "Joe?"

He reached for her bags. "Can I help?" He took two of them and followed her down the hall toward her apartment. "We have to talk," he said.

"Do we?" She walked ahead of him and put one of the bags on the floor, reached into her purse and pulled out a set of keys. She looked back at Joe, smiled, and pushed open the door.

Joe followed her into her apartment with the bags in his arms.

She pointed toward the table. "Put them there," then walked ahead into the kitchen. "So what is it?" she said. "You said we have to talk?"

Joe walked in and stood behind her. "Have you heard from your sister?"

She had placed a couple of cans from her grocery bag up in the cabinet in front of her, then turned to Joe. "Scarlett?"

He paused. "You have another sister?"

"By blood? Yes. But we haven't spoken in years." She raised an eyebrow and huffed out a slight laugh. "You think Scarlett gets herself into trouble? You haven't met Dawn."

"Dawn?"

Morgan nodded. "But no. I haven't heard from Scarlett. Not since I told you I followed her to the apartments." She looked down. "I'm sorry about your friend."

"How'd you know he was my friend?"

She stared back at him, then shrugged. "Wasn't he?"

Joe didn't bother to answer. And he wondered if she knew what happened to Matthew's cousin. Or why she hadn't mentioned it.

He leaned with his hands on the back of a chair tucked under the small round table in front of him. "What I need to tell you... I'm not one hundred percent certain is true. But something's happened."

She swallowed hard and stopped what she was doing to focus on Joe. "Scarlett?"

He stared back at her. "Dickie got home from, well, wherever he was, found a note on the door. Your sister's been kidnapped."

Morgan sucked in half the air in the room with a gasp, covered her mouth with both hands, her eyes wide open. "Scarlett? She's been kidnapped? Is that all there is? A note?"

"So far, yes. But, like I said, I'm not completely convinced."

"I don't understand. You don't believe something's happened to her? What did... what did the cops say?"

Joe shook his head. "Dickie hasn't called the cops."

Morgan grabbed on to the back of the chair on the other side of the table and eased herself into it. She put her head in her hands, her elbows up on the table. "I'm sorry, Joe. I know you think she's up to something. But we have to call the police. We can't just—"

"The note said not to. Or else... or else something bad would happen to Scarlett."

Morgan stared back at him.

"But that's not the only reason," Joe said.

"For not calling the cops?" she said.

"I'm sorry, Morgan. But I'm not buying it."

"Not buying *what?*"

"That she's not involved in something here. That she's a victim."

"Your friend's going to ignore the note? Because, for some reason, you believe it's not real? That she's not in real *danger?*"

"We're not ignoring it. And this is me talking. I haven't said a word about my suspicions to Dickie. He wouldn't believe it either. And he's prepared to do what he has to, to make sure she's back safe."

Morgan stood up from the table. "I'm calling the police." She reached for her phone.

"If you're willing to have your own sister's blood on your hands, then go right ahead."

"Why would I have—"

"I told you. Whoever left the note made it clear not to get the cops involved."

Morgan froze a moment, then looked at the phone in her hand.

Joe watched her and waited until she put it back on the counter. He wasn't about to explain why he thought it could all be a scheme to extort money from Dickie, going all the way back to the night she first approached him at the bar.

Morgan walked to the refrigerator and pulled out a 1.5-liter bottle of pink-colored wine. She held the bottle toward Joe. "I don't know about you, but I need a drink." She reached into the cabinet and pulled out two glasses. "Would you like a glass?"

Joe shook his head. "No, I'm fine. Thank you. But if you have a beer…"

Morgan put one of the wine glasses back and reached into the refrigerator. She gave him a can of Pabst Blue Ribbon. "I don't know if it's any good. I don't drink beer. It's been in there since…"

Joe cracked open the top and took a sip. "I'm going to help find her. I'm sure she's all right."

Morgan held the glass up to her mouth. Before she took a sip, she said, "Why not just offer the money?"

Joe sipped from his beer and looked at her over the can. "If Dickie wants to lose that much money…"

"Lost? Is that what you'd call it? To potentially save my sister's life? Didn't you say he'd do anything for her?"

"He would. Of course. But I told him we need to be sure. I won't let him just drop off a suitcase packed with hundred-dollar bills and walk away."

"But you'd let my sister die?"

Joe held his gaze on her, then shook his head. "Didn't you hear what I said? I'm going to help find her. I made Dickie that promise."

Morgan looked away, put her glass on the counter. She walked toward Joe and moved past him. "Excuse me for a moment." She turned the corner and disappeared down the hall.

He heard a door close and walked from the

kitchen with the beer in his hand. He looked around the room with the TV and couch, then stepped toward the credenza by the door, the one where he first saw the framed photo of Morgan and Scarlett. But the photo was gone.

He turned his gaze down the hall to check on Morgan, then pulled open one of the credenza's drawers. He reached in and pulled out a small photo album. He placed it on top and flipped through the pages. Right away, he noticed the photos inside the sleeves.

They were Polaroids.

He heard a knob turn and slid the album back into the drawer and hurried into the kitchen. He turned and smiled at Morgan as she came around the corner.

She had a phone in her hand.

He didn't think much of it at first. But also couldn't help but wonder if she'd gone to make a call. Or send someone a text. Maybe even to Scarlett. He kept his eye on her as she walked to the counter and picked up her glass of wine.

Joe said, "You know, I was just thinking. Maybe you're right. The best thing to do, to make sure your sister's safe, is maybe suggest to Dickie he pay the hundred grand." He stared into her eyes as he said it. And he could see the look on her face.

"One hundred grand? Are you sure that's all they wanted?"

Joe almost had to fight back a smile, threw back

the can of beer and finished what was left. He placed it on the table and turned for the door. "Thanks for the beer. Just do me a favor. If you hear from your sister, let me know. I'll go talk to Dickie, see if he's prepared to pay the money."

She stared back at him, a confused look plastered on her face, and nodded.

He headed for the door, walked out into the hall and closed it behind him. He wanted to look back at the peephole, had little doubt she was on the other side watching him.

28

JOE SAT IN the Jeep outside Lauren's apartment, watched her walk toward him dressed nicer than she normally had. Other than the night they first went out together on what clearly turned out to be a date. He still couldn't wrap his mind around the way he looked at her now, even after all those years where having any kind of romance with her never crossed his mind.

She stepped up into the Jeep. "How's he doing?"

Joe shrugged and shifted the Jeep into drive. "I haven't seen him yet." He took off out of the parking space onto Northeast First Avenue, headed toward I-395 West. "He's worried, of course. And I'm not sure exactly what to tell him."

He kept his eyes on the road but could feel Lauren watching him.

"What about you?" she said. "Are you worried?"

Joe waited before he answered. "You mean, that

I'm wrong? And it turns out she gets killed because I don't believe she was actually kidnapped?" He scratched his neck and looked straight ahead, turning to her again. "That wouldn't be good, would it." He kept his eyes on her, then looked up into the rearview and kept them on the white sedan he thought he saw earlier. He took the exit for Northwest Thirty-Seventh, merged onto Northwest Fourteenth and had his eyes back in the rearview, but the car was gone.

"I thought we were going to Dickie's?" Lauren said, then followed Joe's eyes in the rearview and turned in her seat, looked out the rear of the Jeep.

"Just gotta make a quick stop to see Juan Pedro."

"The pawnshop?"

Joe nodded, turned left onto South Le Jeune Road and over to Northwest Seventh. He had his eyes along the side of the road, hoping to catch an empty parking space. "It's impossible to find a place to park around here."

"You want to pull over? I'll sit behind the wheel and wait for you."

Joe gave her a quick look. "You sure?"

She nodded. "But are you going to tell me what you're doing here? I'm sure it's not for another Barbara Streisand painting."

He spotted a parking space ahead, almost underneath the awning at La Estella de Oro. He pulled ahead and backed the Jeep up into the space. "You might as well come inside."

They both stepped out and walked toward the store.

Joe pulled the door open for Lauren and looked inside.

Juan Pedro was behind the counter with pliers in his hand. He appeared to be working on a gold chain of some sort and looked up when the bell over the door rang.

Joe and Lauren walked to the counter, but Juan didn't have the same smile on his face like he did the first time Joe had visited to buy a gun.

Joe stepped up to the glass display case between them, and Lauren stopped and looked at the knickknacks on the shelves along the wall to the right.

"Juan," Joe said and turned behind him. "You remember Lauren?"

Juan finally smiled and frisked Lauren with his eyes. "Of course. Of course. But you look different, no?"

"I hope you don't mean it in a bad way," she said with a slight smile, then turned her eyes back to the shelves.

"No, ma'am. No, not at all." He kept his eyes on her, then turned to Joe. "I don't know exactly what happened, other than what I've heard, but I thought you wanted a gun for protection, no?"

Joe shook his head. "I didn't kill him. It's all just a big mistake."

Juan stared back at him. "I didn't think so. But the

cops came by to talk to me… because I sold you the gun, and—"

"I'm sorry for any trouble, Juan. I hope you believe me. I don't have the gun."

"The cops have it?"

Joe shook his head. "No, I was jumped. A couple of guys knocked me out. I woke up and the gun was gone."

"Ju still got the Mossberg?"

"I do. But it's kind of hard to keep in my pants." He smiled, turned, and looked toward the door. "It's actually under the back seat in that Jeep out there."

"What happened to the Mercedes?"

Joe looked down through the glass at the other pistols. "I don't have it anymore."

"What do you need, my friend? I don't see you for all those years, and now…"

Joe looked Juan in the eye. "I need another gun."

Juan opened his mouth to say something, but didn't respond for a few moments. "I'm sorry, Joe. But I can't sell you a gun. You know that, don't you?"

"I do. But I'm hoping you can help me out." Joe turned and glanced back at Lauren, standing behind him now.

Juan shrugged. "I'm sorry. These guns are all accounted for. I can't take the risk. I lose my business. I hope ju understand." He put his hand flat against his chest. "I'm an honest businessman."

"I know you are," Joe said. "But I'm asking for

your help. It's life or death, Juan. I've got people who want to kill me. The same people who took the Glock… shot that man." He glanced back at Lauren, then leaned on the top of the display case. "Juan, you wouldn't want something to happen to Lauren, would you?"

Juan squinted his eyes a bit and looked at Lauren. "What if Miss Lauren makes the purchase?"

Joe shook his head. "We don't have three days to do it by the book. In fact, we don't have three hours."

Juan looked at the pistols on the other side of the glass. He took a deep breath and exhaled, blew his cheeks out wide. He glanced over his shoulder, then turned back to Joe. "We're on camera here. And I can't give you any of these, anyway." He looked to his side, toward a curtain closed across a doorway behind the counter. "Go around to the back of the building. I'll meet you out there. Just go out front, turn left, and walk down the alley between the buildings. I'll be around the corner."

Joe took Lauren by the arm, led her out the front door. They turned left and went between the buildings, stepping over water-soaked cardboard and wooden pallets stacked against the brick wall.

"Are you sure about this?" Lauren said.

Joe didn't answer. He turned around to the back and Juan was already there with the steel-grate door open, waiting for them in the doorway.

Juan stuck his head out and looked back and

forth along the back of the building, then handed Joe a black velvet-like bag.

Joe reached out for it. It was heavy, especially compared to the Glock. He started to reach into the bag.

"Don't take it out here," Juan said. "I don't know who could be watching." He looked back and forth again. "I've had this one for a long time, my friend. It's not new. Maybe thirty years old."

"What is it?" Joe said. He tucked it under his shirt and stuck the whole thing, still in the bag, inside his pants.

"It's a Colt 1911. A vet brought it in, said it was his from Vietnam." He nodded toward Joe's pants. "Called the *Colt Government.*"

Joe wanted to take it out and have a look, but he didn't. "It still shoots, yeah?"

Juan said, "Single action, semiautomatic, magazine fed. It's a recoil-oriented pistol, chambered for the .45."

Joe didn't know what any of that meant but reached out and shook Juan's hand. "How much?"

Juan waved his hand, his palm out toward Joe. "Stay safe, my friend." He pulled the door closed. It clanked three times when he locked it from the inside.

29

JOE HAD THE Colt in the Jeep's center console still in the velvet bag. He looked up in the rearview and kept his eyes there, almost certain the same white car was behind them that he saw earlier. But it was hard to tell, and he had no idea what kind of car it was.

Lauren looked back. "Is something wrong?" She glanced back over her shoulder once more.

He reached into the center console and pulled out the Colt.

"Joe? What's going on? Is someone back there?" This time, she didn't turn to look. "Joe?"

He looked in the rearview, then glanced at her and shook his head. "It's nothing."

Lauren slouched in the passenger seat and turned to the side-view. Joe watched her, trying to get a look behind them.

"I told you, it's nothing."

She straightened up and turned to him. "That white car was behind us earlier. I saw you looking at it when we were on Biscayne Ave." She leaned her head slightly out the side of the Jeep, her eyes on the side-view.

Joe was tempted to play dumb, tell her he hadn't seen a thing, just so she wouldn't worry. But she wasn't a fool. "Keep your head inside, will you?" He looked up in the rearview and turned onto Southwest Seventeenth.

The white car—a Buick, from what he could tell—drove past them and continued onto 152nd Street.

Joe turned to Lauren, relieved and with a smile. "See? Told you it was nothing."

Dickie stood in the driveway with his cell phone in one hand and what looked like his home phone in the other. He walked toward Joe and Lauren as they both stepped out from the Jeep. "Whose is this?"

Joe walked toward him. "The Jeep? It's Will's."

"Where's the Mercedes?"

He realized he hadn't told Dickie anything about it. "Don't worry about it. It's not important," he said. He reached his arm out toward Lauren. "Dickie, you remember Lauren?"

Dickie looked her over. "Lauren? From the paper?" He turned to Joe. "She looks so different."

Lauren rolled her eyes and continued past them

both. Joe and Dickie followed, and the three went inside the house.

Dickie walked away from them, came right back with an envelope in his hand, gave it to Joe. "The Polaroid's in there, too."

Joe reached into the envelope and pulled out the Polaroid. He looked at the photo of Scarlett in a chair, a rope around her hands in front of her, and a red cloth of some sort over her mouth. He flipped to the back of the photo.

"You want to read the letter?" Dickie said, watching Joe study the picture.

Joe handed the Polaroid to him. "She doesn't look overly distressed, does she?" He took the letter out of the envelope and skimmed over it. It'd been typed and printed from a computer. He looked closer at the watermark etched into the paper. With his eyes down, he said to Dickie. "No word yet?"

Dickie held up the two phones in his hand. "I don't even know what number they're going to call. But, no. Nothing." He turned and nodded toward the room with the car-sized TV up on the wall. The glass coffee table in front of the couch had a black leather briefcase on top of it. "I know you said not to. But I already went and got the three hundred G's."

Joe was surprised and showed it on his face. "You got three hundred grand out of the bank?" He glanced at Lauren, her eyes as wide as his.

Dickie let out a slight laugh. "The bank?" He

shook his head and the smile left his face. "Oh, you're serious?"

Joe let it go. "The thing is, we need to think this through before you even consider handing that money over. I think we should wait it out." He looked at the letter in his hand. "We have forty-eight hours."

Dickie shook his head and looked at his watch. "Not anymore."

Joe knew they'd lost some time. "We have time. Let's not jump to—"

"I told you," Dickie said. "I'll do anything for Scarlett... to keep her safe and get her back with me, where she belongs."

Joe and Lauren gave each other a look. He wanted to tell Dickie what he really thought of Scarlett. And how he was sure this was nothing more than a ploy to get money out of Dickie so she could, Joe assumed, run off with her boyfriend, Matthew Doyle.

"Where was Scarlett when this happened?"

"What do you mean where was Scarlett?" He shrugged. "She was right here. She asked me to go to the store for her. And to the dry cleaners."

"Since when do you pick up the dry cleaning? I thought you had someone who—"

"I got rid of Nicky a couple of weeks ago. Scarlett'd normally pick it up, but..." He looked up at Joe. "What's that matter? I can't pick up my own dry cleaning?"

Joe gave Lauren a quick glance, and he was sure she knew what was going through his head. It was almost obvious. But maybe not to Dickie. "So she sent you out? Gave you a list of things to do?"

Dickie shrugged and nodded at the same time. "I guess so. Yeah." He squinted his eyes and looked at Joe. "I hope you're not trying to say this is something she pulled together." He shook his head. "She wouldn't do something like this." He glanced at Lauren and said it again. "She wouldn't do something like this." He pointed with his thumb toward Joe, with a somewhat crooked smile, his eyes still on Lauren. "He's got *some* imagination, huh? Lets that thing run wild sometimes."

"Dickie, I'm trying to help you," Joe said.

The three hadn't moved from the front door.

Joe reached inside the envelope and pulled out the Polaroid again. He flipped it over to the back and pulled it close to his face. He squinted, then looked back and forth between Dickie and Lauren. "There's a time stamp on here." He handed it to Lauren. "Can you see what time it says?" He turned to Dickie. "What time did you get back?"

Dickie at first looked like he wasn't sure. "A little before noon. Before I called you."

Joe pulled out his phone and flipped through a couple of calls. He saw it was eleven thirty-eight when Dickie had called him.

Lauren handed him the Polaroid. "It's not that clear, but it looks like it says eight forty-seven." She paused a moment. "P.M." She looked Joe in the eye.

He turned to Dickie. "Was she here last night?"

Dickie held his gaze on Joe before he answered, then slowly shook his head. "She… she went out."

"You know what time?"

He looked toward the couch. "I took a nap, fell asleep on the couch watching the news. So maybe six thirty. I woke up, she wasn't here." Dickie had his eyes on the photo in Joe's hand. "We have no way of knowing if the time on the back of that photo's correct, do we?"

Joe thought about the photo album at Morgan's, and the Polaroid shots inside. But he kept it all to himself. For Dickie's sake.

"But she was home early. I mean, she was next to me in bed." He shook his head. "She wasn't abducted last night. I can tell you that."

Joe gave Lauren a look, almost felt bad Dickie still hadn't exactly put it all together the way they had. He knew Dickie well enough he'd be insulted if Joe accused him of being naïve, not knowing this young woman had likely been planning to scam Dickie well before the first time he'd laid eyes on her.

But he had to speak up.

He wrapped his hand around Dickie's upper arm, walked him over to the couch and sat him down in the middle. Joe sat on one side of him and Lauren sat on the other.

"Dickie," he said. "Listen, uh, I know how much you love Scarlett, but…" He hesitated, just to gather his thoughts. "I'm afraid Scarlett's playing you."

Dickie stared at Joe, then turned and gave Lauren a quick look. He stared straight ahead, looked up at the wide-screen TV on the wall, the volume lowered. He turned to Joe with a sleepy look to his eyes. "You mean... you mean... Are you trying to say she wasn't actually abducted? That she—"

"She set you up. And it looks like this guy Matt Doyle and his friends are involved. And her sister."

Dickie kept his stare on Joe. "Which one?"

"Which one *what*?" Joe said.

"Which sister?"

"Morgan. I thought she was the normal one at first. But I get the feeling she hasn't been straight with me at any point. Like she set me up, sent me down to those apartments." He picked the picture up from the coffee table. "And she had a photo album; half the pictures were Polaroids." Joe got up, looked at the briefcase on the coffee table beneath them. "And when I left her apartment, I told her the note said it was a hundred grand."

"But it was three hundred," Dickie said.

"I know. But I wanted to see if I could get a reaction. And I did. She almost dropped her glass, said she thought it was more than that. But I never said a word about how much it was supposed to be."

Dickie got up and walked across the room, stood near the front door, and looked out through the glass storm door. With his back to Joe and Lauren, he said, "I don't know if I buy it. I mean, I get why you would think that…" He turned from the door. "But it doesn't all add up, you ask me."

"All I'm saying is we can't take any chances." He nodded toward the briefcase. "Unless you don't care to lose three hundred grand, just give me some time."

Dickie looked at his watch, then looked up at Joe. "We don't have much of it, Joey. But what if you're wrong, and something happens to her?"

30

JOE SAT IN the Jeep, parked far enough away from the entrance to the Mayan Tower Apartments. He had the binoculars he bought from La Estrella de Plata up against his eyes. Although it was dark outside, he slouched low in the seat to avoid being seen.

He doubted Matt Doyle would show his face, or any of the others he knew might've been involved in Scarlett's so-called abduction. But he'd hoped to see something, anything, that might give him some answers. Going to Morgan's made little sense, unless he wanted to confront her and get her to admit she knew more than she'd let on. But why bother? She seemed to have no problem lying to his face.

He looked at the analog clock on the Jeep's dashboard. It was ten past ten. He'd already been outside for four hours. Twenty-three people had gone in and out of the apartment's entrance. Not one was Matt Doyle or Idél or Eugene. He turned and looked back at the other cars parked on the street behind him.

His phone buzzed and he answered right away. His voice was hushed. "Dickie?"

"I just got the call. They said I want her back, it'll take another two hundred G's."

"On top of the three?" Joe said. "Half a million?"

"You believe these sons of bitches?"

"I'll be honest, Dickie. I wondered why they only asked for three in the first place. If there are three or four of them involved, three hundred grand doesn't exactly give you a score to retire on." Joe thought about the last thing he'd said to Morgan before he left her apartment and planted the seed. He said, "What did you say? I hope you played it right."

"Yeah, yeah, I did. But I wanted to say they were full of shit."

Joe had the binoculars in his lap but tried to keep his eyes on the front entrance to the apartment. "You gotta try and play it cool when they call, be sure we got this right before—"

"I thought you said she was safe?"

Joe swallowed. "I still believe that. But as soon as I get what I need, we can call their bluff. Until then... just do whatever they say."

"You think I should go get the other two hundred?"

A blonde woman leaving the apartments caught

Joe's eye. Without the binoculars, he swore it was Scarlett. He held the phone between his chin and shoulder, raised the binoculars to his eyes and tried to get a closer look.

"Joe, you still there?" Dickie said.

"Hang on, will you?" Joe put the phone on the passenger seat next to him. He adjusted the focus on the binoculars.

It wasn't Scarlett. But she looked a lot like her. Heavier. A little older. But he recognized the face. He followed her with the binoculars as she walked along the walkway toward the parking lot.

Then it hit him. He knew exactly who it was. He picked up the phone. "It's the nurse."

"What nurse?" Dickie said.

"The one who was with Will when he was shot... then disappeared."

He continued to follow her with the binoculars in one hand, the phone up to his ear with the other.

She continued across the parking lot and stopped on the sidewalk along Seventy-Fourth. She appeared to be waiting for someone.

"Let me call you back," Joe said.

"But what do I tell them if they call back with the place and time we're supposed to meet? That I have the money?"

"No. Tell them you need more time. See if you can stall them."

Joe kept the binoculars up and watched the woman, then pulled his key from the ignition. "I'll call you back." He hung up and stepped from the Jeep.

He walked toward the woman and picked up his pace. But he was barely halfway there when a white car pulled up in front of her on Seventy-Fourth. It looked to be the same car that had followed Joe and Lauren.

The woman reached for the passenger door and stepped inside.

Joe turned around and ran for the Jeep. He jumped inside and slid the key in the ignition. He turned over the engine and drove straight toward Seventy-Fourth and followed the white car onto Fifty-Ninth Avenue.

He didn't want to get too close, but he wasn't about to lose them.

The car drove the speed limit—or close enough —and drove underneath the highway, turned northeast onto Ponce de Leon Boulevard.

Joe hung back just enough, but another car pulled out before he could do anything and got between them. Then another car pulled out in front of that one.

He wished he'd at least gotten the license plate. But with the two cars in front of him, it was almost impossible to see.

Joe kept his eyes on the Buick ahead of him and reached for his phone. He tapped the screen to make a call.

Not even a full ring and someone answered.

"Officer Cannon."

"Bart, it's Joe."

Bart said, "What'd you do *now*?"

Joe didn't answer. "Listen, can you run a plate for me?"

"Run a plate? Are you serious? I'm kind of in the middle of—"

"You know that so-called nurse? The one who supposedly helped Will?"

"The one who disappeared?" Bart said.

"She's a couple of cars ahead of me. I spotted her outside the Mayan Tower Apartments, got in a white Buick I'm sure is the same one that followed me and Lauren."

Bart sighed into the phone. "Joe, I—"

"Please, Bart."

It took him a moment before he answered. "Give me the plate. I'll need a little time."

Joe tried to keep up with the car. They drove past the university and headed west onto Granada Boulevard toward Coral Gables. One of the two cars between them turned off and left just the one between them.

"You going to give me the plate or not?" Bart said.

"Hang right there," Joe said. He tried to find a way to get around the car in front of him, at least to get a view of the plate. "I have another car in my way."

"Can't you go around him?"

He followed the cars past Granada Park. The inside of the Jeep lit up so bright it blinded him. He looked up into the rearview but couldn't see anything but the lights from the car behind him.

The car ahead turned off and Joe hit the gas to catch up with the Buick. But the car behind him stayed close. "Okay, you ready?" he said.

"I have been."

"The first letter is—"

Before Joe could get a word out, his body jerked forward, and his head whipped down and back against the headrest. The car behind him drove straight into the rear of the Jeep. He swerved and almost lost control but straightened out the wheel. He'd dropped the phone and didn't bother to reach for it, somewhere by his feet.

The car behind hit him in the rear again. This time he skidded across the boulevard and onto the lawn of a giant, sprawling ranch home. He'd lost control, drove straight, cut the wheel, turned toward the home's circular driveway, and crashed into a statue inside a well-lit fountain.

He'd stopped and turned to look toward the road. The car that had hit him was still out in the road. Joe reached into the center console and pulled out the Colt he'd gotten from Juan. He ducked behind the backrest of the driver's seat and looked out the rear toward the road.

The car turned toward him and drove fast across the grass. But it stopped a good fifty yards away.

A shot was fired. Joe felt it right away when his shoulder jerked back. The warmth of his own blood soaked into his shirt. He raised the Colt and fired back toward the car without even taking aim, somehow hit a window, and shattered the glass.

The car reversed at full speed, hit the road, and spun into a one-eighty. It took off down the road and disappeared into the darkness.

Joe straightened out in the seat and placed the Colt in his lap. He reached for his shoulder, then looked at his bloody hand in the light from the fountain.

The lights inside and outside the house all came on at once, lit the yard up like a football field.

The Jeep had stalled, but Joe turned the key to start the engine and it revved. He shifted into reverse and slammed his foot on the gas, spun it around and smashed through a short stone wall, made it out to the road and headed west on Granada.

His phone rang from somewhere by his feet. He saw the light from the screen and leaned toward the floor and reached for the phone. "Bart?"

"What the hell just happened?"

Joe had the Jeep doing eighty, hoping he hadn't lost the Buick. It took him a few seconds to answer. "I've been shot."

"Shot? Jesus Christ, Joe. Where? I mean, where the hell are you?"

"Granada Boulevard." Joe held the phone

between his good shoulder and his ear, had his bad arm on the steering wheel and tried to stop the bleeding with his other hand. "Shit, this hurts."

"You gotta tell me, Joe. Where on Granada Boulevard?"

"I'm looking for the Buick. Another car drove me off the road."

"Don't be an idiot. Just get yourself to the hospital. The ER."

"It's not that bad," Joe said. Although he didn't believe it himself. And as soon as the words left his mouth he started to feel faint. He let go of his shoulder to look at his hand. There was quite a bit of blood, and it had dripped down his arms. "I... I don't feel too good," he said.

"Give me a landmark. I'm on my way. Call nine-one-one, give them your exact location."

Joe couldn't focus. A couple of cars drove past him and the lights were nothing but blurred. He let up on the gas and pulled over to the side of the road. "I'm at the corner of University Drive, and..." His mouth went dry. He had pain in his stomach. "I'm going to see if I can make it to the hospital."

"You must be near Coral Gables?"

Joe pulled back onto the road. He dropped the phone and didn't bother to pick it up. He leaned forward, and did all he could to focus on the road. All he wanted to do was close his eyes and sleep. But he pushed himself and drove another mile, turned into the parking lot at the ER at Coral Gables Hospital and stopped at the entrance. He left the key in the ignition and stepped out. He stumbled and made it through the sliding doors, then fell to the floor as soon as he was inside.

31

BART WAS SEATED in the waiting room at Coral Gables Hospital when Joe walked out with his arm in a sling.

"Looks like I'm going to live," Joe said with a slight smile and continued toward the automatic sliding door at the entrance. He stopped and turned to Bart, walking just behind him. "You ever been shot?"

Bart shook his head. "Knock on wood."

Joe waited for him to catch up. "Well, it hurts, you know."

They stepped outside onto the sidewalk and Bart turned to Joe. "Found the bullet."

Joe winced and straightened out his back, like he was trying to loosen up a kink. "I thought the doctor was going to tell me it was somewhere inside me. But it went in and out." He stepped off the curb but couldn't remember where he'd parked the

Jeep.

"You were lucky, Joe," Bart said. He held out a plastic bag, showed Joe the bullet inside. "It was there on the floor of the Jeep. Went through the back of your seat, apparently right through you, hit the radio but didn't have enough left to penetrate the plastic." He smiled. "Lucky for the radio, you were in the way."

Joe took the bag and held it up under the streetlight in the parking lot. "So where was it?"

"On the floor, on the passenger side."

"Can you do anything with it? Find a match?"

"It doesn't work like that, Joe. And I need to be careful. We had our guys at the scene. But I came right here... didn't want to risk having to explain I know who crashed into the homeowner's statue." He took the bag from Joe and turned, looked back toward the building. "Been in that waiting room for four hours."

Joe stopped and stared back at Bart. "You didn't have to wait."

"Yeah, no shit." Bart continued ahead of Joe.

"Does anyone know you have the bullet?"

Bart shook his head. "No, not yet. I, of course, will have some explaining to do, without getting myself in trouble." He took the bag from Joe. "But, yes, forensics will try to run a match."

They stopped at the front of the Jeep. Joe looked inside, touched his hand to the blood on the back of the driver's seat, but it had dried. "You know what kind of gun it was fired from?"

Bart gave Joe a look. "Like I said, I'll get it into forensics." He held up the bag in front of him. "You can see it's hollowed out. That's why there was so much blood... almost knocked you out. You're just lucky it went all the way through. They usually don't."

Joe stared at the mushroomed bullet inside the plastic bag, then used his good hand to pull himself up into the Jeep.

Bart stepped next to the driver's side, stood just outside next to Joe. He lifted his shirt and showed Joe the Colt Government single-action pistol Joe had gotten from Juan.

Joe looked at it, slid the key in the ignition and turned to Bart. He thought he'd play dumb. "What's that?"

"I was hoping you'd tell me," Bart said.

Joe looked straight ahead through the windshield, toward the front of the Jeep. He waited, then turned to Bart. "You find it in here?" He shrugged. "Must've been Will's."

"I didn't say I found it in the Jeep, did I?"

They both held each other's gaze.

Joe hung his wrist over the steering wheel. "All right," he said. "Can we just keep it between you and me? Maybe put it back where you found it... pretend you never saw a thing?"

He narrowed his eyes at Joe. "You want me to pretend I didn't find an illegal firearm in your vehicle?"

Joe scratched the side of his face with his good hand and slowly nodded. "That would be nice of you." He smirked at Bart.

Bart pulled the Colt from his pants and flipped the handle toward Joe. With a nod, he said, "Gun's got to be forty-something years old. Old Colt like that'd been used in the wars."

Joe reached out from the Jeep and took the gun from Bart. "I've heard."

Bart folded his arms across his chest. "So, you going to tell me what you know? Or do I have to open a full-blown investigation without you? Waste a lot of my time. And yours."

"The nurse I told you about," Joe said. "Whoever she is, if she didn't kill Will, then she knows who did."

"She lives at the apartments?"

Joe thought for a moment. "I assume so. But no way to say for sure. But she's connected to this whole thing."

"The whole thing?" Bart said.

"This scheme... whoever's involved in trying to get money from him."

"Whoa," Bart said. "You mean the guy who owes Dickie money?"

Joe shook his head. "That's just a part of it. There's more." He looked at the badge on Bart's belt. "You put that badge aside for now, maybe I can tell you a little more."

Bart had a look on his face, like he wanted to reach out and grab Joe by the neck. "You'd better start talking, Joe. I don't have patience for your—"

"Bart, please. Okay, okay. Listen…"

Joe stepped out of the Jeep and leaned back against the front fender. He went on and told Bart everything he knew about Scarlett, how she was allegedly kidnapped—and why he didn't believe it—and Matt Doyle and Scarlett's sister and how Idél and Eugene were the ones at Will's office the day Joe got knocked out. He told him about the three hundred grand Dickie had in a suitcase on his coffee table. Plus the additional two hundred the so-called kidnapper demanded if Dickie wanted to save Scarlett.

Bart shook his head when Joe was done talking. "Jesus Christ." He looked off across the parking lot and scratched the back of his head. He turned back to Joe. "I don't know why this is the first I'm hearing about all this, Joe. I mean, I thought we were—"

"I told you at the diner."

He looked off again. "Obviously, you left a few things out. But now I almost wish I hadn't asked." He turned back to Joe and looked him in the eye. "You can't just decide out of the blue you're going to start playing cops and robbers." He took a deep breath and let it all out, still shaking his head. "I'm in somewhat of a bind here, Joe." He leaned with both hands up on the roll bar over the driver's side of the Jeep. "I bring this bullet in… I can't just ask for a favor. It doesn't work like that."

"You've been a cop for, what, fifty years? You must have a friend or two who'll—"

"Don't be a smart-ass. Thirty years. I knew I should've just retired."

"What about the bullet Will was shot with? Can you at least see if there's a match there? Or maybe even the one they pulled out of Daniel Doyle?"

Bart's eyebrows tightened over his eyes. "Now you're going to tell me how to do my job?"

"Just making a suggestion," Joe said.

Bart loosened up the look on his face, cracked a slight smile. "Not a bad one." He looked at his watch. "Four in the morning. A couple hours sleep wouldn't hurt either of us." He turned and headed toward his car but stopped and looked back at Joe. "I still think you should stick to writing. But you probably would've made a decent cop."

32

JOE WOKE UP on the couch in his apartment. He thought about having a drink, but it wasn't even eight in the morning, and he barely had three hours of sleep.

His shoulder was sore but nothing like he'd expected. Although it didn't hurt he took a couple extra pills for the pain. He looked at his phone on the coffee table and thought about calling Lauren but didn't want to get her worried. He was just glad he didn't take her with him.

He dialed her number, but she didn't answer. And a couple of minutes later, he tried again. She could've been sleeping or in the shower. She'd mentioned a job interview, but he didn't know much about it or even what day.

After a few more tries, he had another cup of coffee and changed his clothes, wet his hair and headed out the door with the Colt 1911 tucked in his pants.

Joe used his right hand, his good arm, to reach up and grab the roll bar. He stepped down from the Jeep in front of Lauren's apartment building and looked at his phone. He made sure he hadn't missed her call. But he still hadn't heard from her. He couldn't help but be somewhat worried.

He took the elevator up to her apartment and turned down the hall, pulled out his phone and dialed Lauren. He stood outside her door and didn't knock at first. He held the phone up to one ear, the other ear pressed up against the door.

It was quiet inside.

He hung up the phone, but before he could slip it in his pocket, it rang.

"Lauren?" he said without looking at the screen.

"Joe? It's me."

Joe was sure it was Dickie but took a quick glance at his screen. "Dickie? What are you—"

"They have her." He had a clear shake to his voice.

"Scarlett?"

"Lauren. They have her; she's with Scarlett."

Joe rushed down the hall with the phone up to his ear. "Who? How do you know? Who told you?"

"I don't know who. But the caller, the same one who's already called, said if we want to play games, we'll both be jerking ourselves off with our girlfriends dead."

Joe pushed the button on the elevator and kept his eyes on the arrows above the door. He looked behind him at the stairwell, reached for the handle, and pulled open the door. He raced down the stairs and felt the pain in his shoulder with each step. "Are you at your house?" he said through the bounce in his breath.

"Yeah, but let me tell you something, Joe. They said the price'll keep going up the more you get in the way. And if we want them both alive, it's gone up another hundred grand."

Joe crashed through the door and into the lobby. "Don't do anything until I get there."

"All right, but you gotta hurry. I already have the money. And I've decided I'm giving it to them. I'm not dicking around like this anymore, Joe. I'm not willing to take the chance. I promised I'd be there."

"Be where?"

"At Saint Dominic's."

Joe stopped outside his Jeep, pulled the Colt from his pants, and leaned over the driver's seat. "The church?" He placed the Colt into the center console. He stepped up inside and switched the phone to his left hand. It hurt his shoulder when he first raised his arm, but he'd dealt with worse pain before. He pulled the Jeep's key from his pocket and slid it into the ignition.

"You know where it is?"

"Saint Dominic's?"

"Yeah. You know where it is?"

"Of course. You're not going now, are you?"

"No. Midnight, in the back parking lot."

Joe turned the Jeep around with one hand and headed in the other direction toward Dickie's house. "Hang tight, okay? I'm going to make a quick stop, then I'll be over."

"A quick stop *where?*"

"To see Scarlett's sister Morgan."

Dickie was momentarily quiet on the other end. "You think she knows something?"

"I think she does."

Joe walked along the hall toward Morgan's apartment. He knocked hard so she could hear him but had a feeling she wasn't going to answer even if she was home. He waited, then knocked a second time. He pressed his ear against the door and didn't hear a thing on the other side.

He reached into his pocket and pulled out a small leather, wallet-like case, glanced over his shoulder, then stepped toward the doorknob. He opened the case and removed a lockpick set. It was the same one an old friend had given him after the guy had closed his locksmith business and moved away. He had shown Joe a thing or two about how to pick a lock, but Joe never imagined he'd ever need to.

But he'd practiced a few times and could only hope he could get into Morgan's apartment.

He hadn't noticed any cameras and looked behind him one more time. He crouched low to get a good look at the lock on the knob. He stuck the tension wrench into the lock and remembered his friend telling him, more than once, applying the right amount of pressure with the tension wrench was key to picking the lock. He slid the pick into the lock and raked it back and forth. He eased up on the pressure wrench and continued sliding the pick until he felt the lock turn.

He reached for the knob, turned it and pushed open the door. He was careful as he closed it behind him and stepped inside the apartment. "Morgan?" He turned, reached for the closed door and locked it.

He walked along the hall and studied the framed photos on the wall. Some were of people and children that Joe, of course, wouldn't know. There were landscape photos, one he recognized as South Point Park at sunset. He saw another photo with Morgan and Scarlett seated at an outdoor table with a yellow umbrella over them. They each had a drink in their hand and held them up to the camera.

Joe looked closer and saw a third drink on the table. But then he looked at the two women he thought were Scarlett and Morgan. It wasn't, in fact, Scarlett in the photo. He looked off and pictured the woman who was there when Will had died. He looked back at the photo and knew right then the woman with Morgan was the same woman outside the apartment: the same woman in the white Buick.

He pulled out his phone and snapped a picture of it. He walked back to the credenza with the photo album. He reached into the drawer and pulled it out, flipped through the pages with the Polaroid photos. He hadn't had a chance to look through them all when he was there with Morgan. But this time he saw her picture. She was in some of the photos with Morgan. Some with Scarlett. And in others, with all three of them together.

Joe shook his head in disbelief as he flipped through the pages. He couldn't believe he hadn't recognized her that first time and saw how much she looked like Scarlett. Not enough to be twins, at least not identical, but he had no doubt they were related. He assumed sisters but couldn't be sure.

He closed the album and put it back in the drawer. But before he could turn from the credenza, he heard a click. He put his good hand up, his right hand, and did what he could to raise the arm still in the sling. He turned slowly and looked into the muzzle raised up in front of his face.

"Matt Doyle," he said. "I was wondering when we'd get a chance to meet."

Doyle didn't speak. Not right away. He just held the gun on Joe and stared back at him.

"So, what are you going to do?" Joe said. "Shoot me? Right here in Morgan's apartment?" Joe eased down his hands and felt the sting in his shoulder.

"Keep your hands up," Doyle said.

Joe looked at his left arm. "It's kind of hard with this thing on. I'm sure you know why I have to wear it." But he took his eyes from Matt Doyle and focused on the gun. "Hey! Is that my Glock?"

Doyle shook his head, kept it pointed on Joe. "Not anymore."

"So, what's the story? You in on this with the three sisters? I hope you're not sleeping with all three of them, are you? That'll never turn out well, you know."

Morgan walked around the corner and stood behind Matt. She put one hand on his waist and rested her chin on his shoulder. "He's only sleeping with me," she said, giving Joe a wink as she stepped around to Matt's side.

Joe looked from Morgan to Matt. "What have you done with Lauren?"

Morgan shook her head. "You have nothing to worry about. She's fine. As long as you stay out of our way."

Joe looked into the Glock's muzzle and thought for a second he could reach for the Colt tucked into his pants. He got the feeling this guy Matt wasn't the brightest, just by the stupid look on his face. But you didn't have to be smart to pull a trigger and hit a target four feet in front of you.

"Where's Scarlett hiding?" Joe said.

Matt and Morgan both laughed but neither answered. Morgan turned and walked away toward the kitchen.

Joe looked at the muzzle, then shifted his eyes to Matt. "Is this how you killed your cousin? Close range… with *my* gun?"

Morgan walked toward them with a rope and a roll of duct tape in her hand. But she took the gun from Matt, kept it pointed on Joe.

Doyle took the rope and duct tape and grabbed Joe's bad arm and twisted it behind his back.

Joe let out a scream and saw a spot of blood soak through his shirt from his shoulder. "Jesus Christ, you son of a bitch." He tried to grab Matt with his other hand, but Matt punched him in the back of the head.

"Don't make me have to shoot you, Joe," Morgan said.

Matt twisted him and slammed his head on top of the credenza. He grabbed Joe's wrists and pulled them together, used his free hand to wrap the rope around his arms. He pulled it tight on Joe's wrists, then ran over the rope with duct tape.

With Joe's hands tied up behind his back, he wasn't sure what he'd be able to do. The Colt was still in his waistband, but there was no chance he could pull it out. He wished he already had.

Matt threw him to the floor and tied his ankles with another rope and went over the top with the duct tape at least a dozen times. Then he stepped toward Joe's head, bent down, and tore off another piece of tape. He ran it across Joe's mouth. "Give me a hand," he said to Morgan.

Together they dragged Joe by his feet across the hardwoods and down the hall. They pulled him into a bedroom. The bed had four tall posts, and together they tied Joe to one of them.

"Now be a good boy," Matt said. He pulled out his phone and looked at the screen. "We're meeting Uncle Dickie later tonight!" He turned and walked out of the room.

Morgan followed behind him but stopped at the doorway and turned to Joe. "I'm sorry about this, hon. I sure wish you could've minded your own business. I would've enjoyed getting to know you." She winked at him, pulled the door closed and left the room.

33

JOE LEANED UP against the post they'd tied him to. He was surprised they didn't check to see if he had a gun or that they didn't take his phone. But it wasn't like he could get to either one with his hands tied together.

He didn't get the idea Matt had much upstairs, although he knew how to tie a rope. It was so tight around Joe's wrist his hands ached and his fingers tingled. He turned and looked up at the post he was tied to. It was at least six feet in height and four inches or so thick.

He saw his own reflection in a mirror attached to the wall, with the blood coming from his injured shoulder.

The phone in his pocket rang, but there was no way he could answer it. He looked up at the post and tried to think of a way to break free. The ringing stopped, but the sound he'd set for texts followed.

He tried to push himself up along the post to get to his feet. But the rope around the post wouldn't budge. But he didn't give up. He used his feet and pushed himself to an almost seated position.

He pushed more until he was almost straightened out. But not quite.

He looked up at the post, took a deep breath and drove his shoulder into it. The pain shot through his shoulder: his *good* shoulder.

In the process, the rope seemed to loosen somewhat. And he was able to pull away from the post and get more momentum. He again drove his shoulder into the post with every ounce of strength he could muster.

He had to stop to let the pain subside.

He tried again, this time got more of his body into it, hit the post with his shoulder and heard a crack.

The problem was, Joe didn't know for sure if the sound came from the post or his shoulder.

He leaned against the post with his forehead and tried to catch his breath.

His phone rang, but there was still nothing he could do to answer it. Not unless he could somehow get his hands free. Without another thought he slammed his shoulder into the post. And this time the crack was distinct. He knew it didn't come from his shoulder. He hit it again and could see the post was cracked. He hit it again and did all he could to ignore the pain he felt every time he made impact.

But he heard someone pound on the door to the apartment. At least he thought he did. He stopped slamming his shoulder into the post and listened. He wished he had the Colt in his hand.

There was a crash, followed by someone's voice. Footsteps grew louder outside the bedroom door.

"Joe? You in here?"

It was Bart. But Joe couldn't answer him with the duct tape over his mouth. But he tried. "Mmmm."

The door swung open. Bart stood in the doorway with his gun drawn, tucked it into his holster and rushed across the room. He ripped the tape from Joe's face. "You the only one here?"

Joe stretched his mouth and tried to speak but nothing came out. He cleared his throat. "They have Lauren. And they're going to meet Dickie at midnight." He watched Bart pull out his knife and cut away the rope. "How'd you know I was here?" The rope and duct tape fell off his wrists.

"I called Dickie. He said you went to see his girlfriend's sister. He told me about Lauren."

Joe nodded. "I still don't know if Dickie's girlfriend's involved in this scheme, or if she really has been abducted by her sisters."

"Sisters? I thought it was just the one," Bart said.

"She's got two sisters. One of 'em's the one in the Buick. The same woman who was there when Will was killed." Joe looked up at the post and Bart cut the rope from his ankles.

"The sister did this to you all by herself? Tied you up?" He made a face. "Tough lady."

"No, she was with Matt Doyle. That's why I'm not sure about Scarlett. I thought she was together with him. Turns out her sister stepped in. And now it makes sense why she sent me down to those apartments with Will."

They both started toward the door, but Joe turned back and walked up to the bedpost. He threw his shoulder into it and watched it crash onto the floor. He turned and walked past Bart without a word.

On the way past the credenza, he opened the drawer and pulled out the photo album, handed it to Bart. "All three sisters' photos are in there."

They walked out together and down the hall, stood quiet in front of the elevator and watched the arrows above the door.

"How'd you know I was in trouble?" Joe said.

Bart shook his head and glanced toward Joe. "I didn't. Not right away." He paused a moment. "I was looking for you, to let you know you've been cleared of Daniel Doyle's murder."

Joe opened his eyes wide. He was in pain, but it seemed to clear a bit once those words came out of Bart's mouth. "How? What'd you do?"

"The bullet they removed from Daniel Doyle matched the one you were hit with. That's all they needed."

The elevator doors opened and they both stepped inside.

Bart pulled out a pack of gum and stuck a piece in his mouth. "Oh, and I'm being suspended," he said. He held the pack of gum out toward Joe.

Joe waved him off. "Suspended? Jesus, Bart. I'm sorry. Is it—"

"Not your fault. But not reporting your little incident, and the missing gun…"

"I didn't tell you about the gun until…"

"If I didn't come clean, you wouldn't have been cleared. So, let's just call it a decent trade-off." He shrugged. "I don't mind taking the time off."

"Shit," Joe said. "I'm sorry. Really."

The elevator doors opened, and they both stepped off and walked out the glass door toward the street.

Bart's car was parked behind the Jeep.

"I have to get to Dickie's," Joe said.

"You want me to drive?" Bart said.

"Maybe you shouldn't be involved from here, Bart. I think I've gotten you in enough trouble."

"I'm not going to let you go out there by yourself." He gave Joe a nod. "Look at you. You're lucky you're not dead."

"But they told Dickie… no cops involved. And now it's not just Dickie's girlfriend we have to worry about."

They both stood in silence.

"You gotta let me help you, Joe," Bart said.

Joe hesitated. "You can't call it in though, Bart. You have to put your badge away."

Bart huffed out a slight laugh. "What the hell do you think it means when you get suspended?" He lifted his jacket and showed Joe his empty belt. "They took my badge already."

Joe called Dickie from the Jeep. He tried his cell phone then his home phone, but Dickie didn't answer. He looked up in the rearview mirror at Bart, just behind him in the blue Crown Victoria. He stuck his arm out and waved for Bart to pull up next to him.

Joe pulled the Jeep off into the grass along the side of the breakdown lane and made room for Bart to pull over.

Bart put down the passenger side window and leaned over the empty passenger seat. He looked out toward Joe. "Everything all right?"

"Dickie didn't answer his phones."

"Aren't we almost at his house?"

Joe didn't answer, had his hand rested up on the steering wheel and looked straight ahead. He turned back to Bart. "I'm just afraid they went to him. They weren't supposed to meet until midnight. And I get the feeling Doyle and Scarlett's sister were anxious to get their hands on that money."

"I'm not following, Joe. Then why are we stopped? Let's get to his house before—"

"We need to be prepared to run into something we might not be expecting."

"They think you're tied up to a bed. Isn't that enough of a surprise?"

"I think we park a block away or so. Cut through the yard behind Dickie's."

"But you have no idea if anyone's with him?"

"No idea at all. I can't think of a reason why they'd leave Dickie without killing him."

34

JOE TURNED ONTO Colonial Drive and drove past Kings Grant Park to Southwest 152nd, turned and parked on 161st Street. He stepped out of the Jeep and watched Bart drive past him and stop a good twenty or so feet ahead of him.

Bart got out of his Crown Victoria and popped the trunk, reached inside, and came up with a harness with two pistols already in each harness. He slipped it over his back and reached into the trunk again and grabbed a third handgun. He tucked it into the front of his pants and walked toward Joe at his Jeep.

Joe said, "I guess you came prepared?" He walked around to the back of the Jeep, lifted the rug and the plastic cover over the storage compartment. He pulled out the Mossberg 500. He had the Colt tucked in his pants.

Bart said, "Didn't you say you hadn't fired that

thing yet?"

Joe shrugged with a crooked smile. "First time for everything."

Bart looked off toward the houses along the street. "I just hope this doesn't turn into a bloodbath." He turned his eyes back to Joe. "Especially if it's our blood."

The houses in the neighborhood were mostly larger than what Joe had always considered normal. Most of the homes looked the same, with stucco siding and plush green lawns and flowered landscapes.

Joe and Bart walked another twenty yards along the street, then turned down one of the driveways and between two of the homes. In the back the yards weren't enclosed but divided with what looked like tall areca palms.

"That's Dickie's house, next one over," Joe said. He stuck his head through the trees and put a pair of binoculars up to his face. He looked past the pool and had his eyes on the house. "If they're in there, they'll kill Dickie if they get even the slightest idea I'm out here. Luckily they think I'm out of the picture."

Bart pulled a gun from his holster. "Let's not waste any more time."

They both walked out from the trees and into Dickie's backyard, crouched behind a row of flowering shrubs along the back of the in-ground pool.

Bart reached his hand out. "Give me those binoculars." He took them from Joe and put them up in front of his eyes with one hand, the pistol still in the other.

"You see something?" Joe said.

Bart didn't answer. He moved the binoculars along the back of the house, then handed them back to Joe. "See that window to the right of that door? Someone's standing there, and it ain't Dickie."

Joe lifted the binoculars and looked along the house and settled on the double doors, moved to the right and without a doubt knew who it was. "Matt Doyle," he said, the binoculars still up in front of him. "He's talking, but I don't see the other person." He turned to Bart. "You think we can get closer?"

Bart stood up from behind the shrubs without saying a word. He took one step, and a gunshot was fired from somewhere inside the house.

"Dickie!" Joe yelled and jumped up from behind the shrub and ran toward the house. He held the Mossberg with both hands and got behind the cabana on the other side of the pool. Bart ran up behind him, but Joe took off for the house without a word.

He ran around the side and out to the front. He stopped at the corner, saw the white Buick, and the BMW Scarlett had been driving.

Idél and Eugene stepped out from the front door but Idél stopped and walked back inside. Eugene kept going and looked toward Joe.

Joe tried to pull back, but it was too late.

Eugene lifted the Glock he'd taken from Joe and fired a shot, followed by two more. Chunks blew off the corner of the house.

Joe lifted the Mossberg, pumped it once and pulled the trigger. But it was the first time he'd ever fired it. The shot went high and wide, hit a palm tree on the other side of the driveway.

Bart shoved Joe out of the way before Eugene could get off another shot. He fired his gun.

Eugene's chest caved and his shoulders slumped forward. He collapsed on the walkway in front of Dickie's front door.

"Now you know why I asked if you'd ever shot that thing," Bart said.

Joe stared at Eugene's lifeless body.

A window opened from behind Joe and Bart. They both turned as Idél stuck his body halfway out of the opening with a pistol in each hand.

He fired just as Joe and Bart ran from the side of the house and headed for the driveway. They both ducked behind the Buick.

A shot was fired, and the Buick's rear window shattered.

Bart and Joe held their fire and gave each other a look, but neither said a word.

Bart got up on his feet and took one step out from behind the Buick. Another shot was fired and his shoulder kicked back. He stumbled and fell on the ground next to Joe.

"Bart!" Joe pulled him back behind the Buick, out of the line of fire. "Where'd it hit you?"

Bart just stared up at him. He dropped his gun to the ground. Blood soaked through the shirt under his jacket. He opened his mouth, but words didn't come out. He closed his eyes.

"Bart," Joe said. "Stay with me." He put his hand on Bart's chest. "Bart?"

Bart opened his eyes. "I'm fine." He pushed himself up into a seated position and leaned with his back against the car.

Joe reached for the gun on the ground and put it in Bart's hand. He stood up from behind the Buick and pumped the Mossberg, walking toward the house. He kept it pointed at the front door and stepped over Eugene. He fired a shot into the door, then kicked it open.

"Dickie!" he yelled. He looked at the empty coffee table and walked to the kitchen. He saw blood on the floor. "Dickie!" He picked up his pace, and as soon as he stepped into the kitchen he looked down.

He'd expected to see Dickie's body. But that's not who it was.

It was Matt Doyle, his eyes still open. But Joe didn't have to look twice to know he was dead. Not with a hole in his head, just above his eyes.

Glass smashed from somewhere in the house. Joe turned with the Mossberg locked and loaded. He walked from the kitchen and back to the other side of the house. He turned the corner into the room with the couches and the TV up on the wall.

Idél had Dickie from behind with a gun to his head, Dickie's neck in the crux of Idél's arm. He dragged Dickie back through the French doors with the broken glass. Idél turned and kicked them open.

They continued outside. Idél said, "Take another step, my friend, and Mr. Dickie's going to have to die."

Dickie cried, "Joe, don't do anything foolish. These guys aren't messing around."

"I can see that," Joe said. He followed them out into the backyard.

"He give me the money," Idél said, "we don't have to have these problems. You see what I mean?"

Joe was confused. Dickie had told him he had the money. But he noticed the suitcase wasn't on the coffee table.

"I told you," Dickie said. "I dropped the money at the church, like you told me to."

Idél appeared to squeeze harder on Dickie's neck. "I told you not to lie to me, old man."

Joe followed after them, the Mossberg up and pointed toward Idél. But he wasn't sure he'd have another lucky shot if he couldn't get close enough. "Where are the women?"

Dickie's voice wasn't clear, with the pressure Idél put on his throat. "I was told they'd be released once I dropped off the money."

Idél pushed the muzzle harder into the fat under Dickie's chin. "I told you, I have the older one."

"Lauren?"

Idél shrugged. "I didn't ask her name."

"What about Scarlett?" Joe said. "She involved in this?"

"Involved?" Idél shook his head. "My friend in there helped her escape. As you can see, I didn't like that too much."

"Matt Doyle? I thought he was your friend?"

"Friend?" Idél laughed, then shook his head. He pressed the gun's muzzle into Dickie. "I want my money."

Joe stepped closer toward Idél and Dickie. "Will you just let him go? You heard him. He doesn't have the money."

Idél had dragged Dickie to the other side of the pool. "You take another step," he said, "and your friend is going to have to die."

A shot was fired.

Joe jumped but lifted the Mossberg, ready to pull the trigger. He was afraid Dickie was dead.

But Idél's grip loosened on Dickie's neck. His gun dropped to the ground. He stumbled away from Dickie, took a few steps, then fell facedown into the pool with a splash.

Blood floated to the surface.

Dickie and Joe both looked at each other, then each looked around. Dickie ran along the pool and into the house.

Joe turned and saw Bart holding himself up with one hand against the corner of the house. His shirt was covered in blood. He held his gun in his other hand, covered in blood, and gave Joe a blank stare. He tucked the weapon into his holster, then dropped to one knee, and collapsed on the ground.

35

BART TRIED TO sit up in the hospital bed when Joe walked through the door but winced and grabbed his neck.

Joe stepped to the side of his bed. "You all right?"

"Looks that way," Bart said. "Just missed a major artery, from what the doctor said. I forget which one… might've said the subclavian or something. Not that I'd know the difference."

"They weren't sure you were going to make it for a bit," Joe said. He put his hand on Bart's good shoulder. "I'm glad you're okay."

Bart smiled half-heartedly, nodded a couple of times, and again reached for his neck. "So what's the story?"

"We found Lauren. She was where Idél said she'd be, which was kind of a surprise." He turned, looked out the window. "But no Scarlett. And no money. Morgan's apartment was empty for the most part. At least her personal belongings."

"But all Idél would admit to was kidnapping Lauren?"

"We didn't get that much out of him. He only lived long enough to tell us where he left Lauren."

"He's dead?"

"I thought you knew that?"

"No. A couple of guys came in from my division, but nobody's told me much at all." He looked up at Joe. "How's Dickie?"

"Sore neck. But he's more worried about finding Scarlett and his six hundred grand. He's pissed he let her pull one over on him. Maybe embarrassed."

"But you still don't know exactly what her involvement is, do you? I mean, it's clear she teamed up with her sisters, but…"

They were both quiet for a couple of moments.

Joe said, "So, how bad is all of this for *you*?"

"I told you, the doctor said it'll be fine. Stitches will come out in ten days."

Joe gave Bart a look, had a feeling he knew what he meant. "I'm talking about your job, Bart."

"Well, I think the worst-case scenario is I get that retirement I should've taken in the first place." He reached for the plastic cup of water on the cart next to him, took a sip and held the cup in his hand. "You know, I used to tell my wife—ex-wife—that once I got shot I'd be out for good." He shrugged and reached for his neck with his free hand. "Didn't comfort her much… telling her that. She still left me."

Joe waited on the couch at Lauren's apartment with a vodka cranberry in his hand resting on his lap while Lauren showered. He stared out the glass door toward the balcony and thought about the three sisters. He couldn't quite figure out at what point they decided to turn on Idél and Eugene. And maybe even Matt Doyle, although he might've just been the body they threw to the sharks.

Lauren walked out of her bedroom with her hair still wet but back in a ponytail. She didn't have any makeup on and wore her big glasses the way she had for as long as Joe had known her.

It wasn't a bad thing at all, Joe thought.

She sat next to him on the couch but didn't say much. She rested her head on his sore shoulder and he jumped.

"Oh, sorry," she said and moved away from him.

He stared at her, but her eyes were somewhere else.

"You okay?" he said.

She took a moment before she answered, then turned to him with a shrug. "I don't know. Are you?"

He hesitated. "I wish I could just let it all go. But I can't stop thinking about it." He sipped his drink and placed the glass on the table in front of him.

"You said Scarlett was there with you. But you couldn't tell if she was being held against her will or not?"

Lauren nodded. "She seemed to be, when I first got there. But I started to wonder if it was just for show. The big guy covered my eyes, tied me up pretty well, and—"

"Eugene?"

"Yes. He told me I wouldn't get hurt if I just kept quiet. He actually apologized to me a couple of times."

"Really?" Joe looked off. "Are we talking about the same man?"

"The photo the police showed me? Yes, that was him. And the little guy."

"But you're sure it was Scarlett? And not someone who might've looked like her?"

"They used her name. But I guess, I don't know. I guess it's possible it was one of her sisters. Either way, she was tied to a chair when I first got there. A small wooden chair. Like an old kitchen chair. Her hands were behind her back, but I can't say for sure if they were tied or not. She didn't say a word to me. Wouldn't look at me or anything for the few minutes before they covered my face. Then the big guy—Eugene?—he took me into another room. So I don't know what happened to her after that." She turned her eyes to Joe's glass. "You want another drink?"

He picked up his drink and finished what was left.

"No, thank you. I think I'll cut back a bit." He got up and stood at the sliding glass door before the balcony with his hands in his pockets and looked outside. He turned to Lauren. "What about Morgan? Would you have known if she was the one tied up? And not Scarlett?"

Lauren paused. "I don't know. Do they look alike?"

Joe shrugged. "They're sisters. But it could've been the other one, too."

"I'm sorry, Joe. I just… I know I'm not being much help, but—"

Joe's phone rang. He grabbed it from the coffee table and answered it immediately. "Dickie?"

"Joey, where are you?"

"I'm with Lauren, at her apartment. What have you heard?"

"She just called."

"Scarlett?"

"Yes. You know what she said?"

"I will as soon as you tell me."

"She said she was sorry."

"Sorry?" Joe laughed. "For taking your six hundred grand? For pulling Lauren in the middle of this, or—"

"Joey, please. Listen for a minute. She whispered on the call, told me they left the area."

"The area?"

"Miami. But she wouldn't tell me where they went."

"Why *would* she tell you? So you could send the cops after her?"

Dickie didn't answer.

Joe thought for a moment and said, "You know where she called from? Was it her own phone?"

"No, it wasn't."

"Is the number on your phone?"

"Why, can you trace it?"

"Me? No. And I can't imagine she'd be dumb enough to call without blocking the number, but..."

Dickie said, "Actually, it was from a nine-oh-four area code. What's that, up northeast? Jacksonville area?"

"You know if it was a landline?"

"How would I know that, Joey?"

"Dickie, I'm trying to help. And you're—"

"I'm being serious. I don't know how to tell if it's a landline or a cell phone these days. Do you?"

"Why didn't you call back the number after she hung up?"

"Oh, I guess I just didn't. I called you. She only called a few minutes ago. I gotta be honest, Joey. I'm tired. I can't even think straight."

The line went quiet.

"Dickie?"

"You know how I felt about her," Dickie said. "I didn't want to believe she would've done something like this to me."

"I know," Joe said. "I get it. But if you want to get your money back, you're going to have to snap out of it. This might be our only chance. Who knows how far they'll go."

Lauren got up and grabbed Joe's glass, went into the kitchen and made them both a drink.

Joe said, "Dickie, how about you call the number on your phone, see who answers? You can just hang up or call me back. You know how to block your number before you call?"

"It used to be star sixty-seven. That still work?"

"It should," Joe said. "Give it a try and call me right back."

Lauren walked over to the couch and sat down, put the two drinks on the coffee table.

The phone rang again and Joe answered. "Dickie?"

"The Amelia Hotel."

Joe shook his head. "No shit, huh?" He glanced at Lauren, then said into the phone, "I know you loved her, Dickie. But you have to admit she wasn't the sharpest knife in the drawer." He sipped his drink. "All right, you need to decide if you want the money back, or do you want Scarlett back."

"I'm not seeing how either would be possible. I mean, she means more to me than money ever would. But even if you found her and dragged her back here, I don't see how things would ever be the same between us."

"Oh, I don't think it would be. But what if, and this is a big IF, what if her sisters are behind all of this, and Scarlett really is a victim. Maybe they're holding her against her will?"

Dickie was quiet for a moment. "You really think that's possible?"

Joe hesitated a moment. He hated to get Dickie's hopes up. But he decided he'd do all he could to help his friend. Of course, part of him wanted his cut of the prize, and he knew Dickie would make good on what they'd agreed to. But with Dickie down to whatever he had left in his wallet, Joe's only hope was to get the money back. If it came with Scarlett attached to it, so be it. "I don't know why else she would have called you if there wasn't more to this than either of us realize."

36

JOE SAT AT Will's old desk in his office after he contacted the landlord of the building where Will worked. The man told Joe that Will received cheap rent in exchange for keeping an eye on the place.

Joe didn't mention to him Will was actually living out of the office. But he did convince the landlord to give Joe the same deal, and then Joe would keep an eye on the place.

Even though Will hadn't paid taxes or business fees to the state, and his business had been automatically dissolved, Joe kept Will's sign up on the wall just outside the door.

Joe typed on his laptop with the door closed. He would normally put his phone on silent whenever he tried to write, but he didn't want to miss out on any business either. Not that he advertised or made anything official. He had no plans to get his private investigator's license but would take jobs as they came and work around a new novel he'd been writing for a couple of weeks.

He'd just about finished chapter two.

He jumped when his phone rang and broke his thought. He looked at the screen and didn't recognize the number. But he needed to start making some money, so he cleared his voice and tried to sound as professional as he could. "Joe Sheldon."

Nobody spoke on the other end.

Joe said, "Hello?"

"Joe, uh, this is Scarlett. I need you to listen to me for a—"

"What a surprise," he said, and leaned back in the office chair. "What's the matter, you already spent all Dickie's money?"

She was quiet for a moment. "*I* didn't. But my sisters are doing a pretty good job of it."

Joe closed the top of his laptop. "I'll admit, you're the last person I expected to hear from."

Scarlett paused again on the other end. "I know you won't believe me, but this wasn't at all how it was supposed to turn out."

Joe laughed. "Even if I had a reason to believe a word coming from your mouth, I'm sure you're enjoying yourself out on some island with your two lovely sisters. Life can't be too bad when you have six hundred grand to play with."

"Will you just listen to me?"

"I'm not sure I have a good enough reason to

listen to anything you say."

"What if I tell you where we are?"

Joe straightened out in the chair and leaned forward on the desk but didn't say a word. He just listened.

Scarlett said, "If you agree to meet me, I'll tell you everything."

"Meet you where? If you're going to tell me to fly across the country, or wherever you ended up, you'll have to at least pay my airfare. That way, I'll know you're serious." He cleared his throat. "And I'm not saying I trust you."

"We're not across the country, Joe. We're up in North Carolina. In Asheville."

"Asheville?"

"We're staying at a house. In the Blue Ridge Mountains."

"The three of you are wanted. All I have to do is call the cops and have the three of you arrested on the spot. So, why would you trust *me*?"

"Because I think you're that kind of guy, Joe. I'm asking for your word, that you won't call the cops. Can I trust you?"

"I guess it depends."

They were both quiet for a moment.

"Okay," Scarlett said, "I'll call you in the morning with more details. I'll purchase your ticket and have it for you at the airport. Someone will be there to pick you up when you land."

Joe was careful before he responded.

"Oh, and Joe," Scarlett said, "please don't tell Dickie I called you. Don't tell anyone. Please. At least not yet."

Joe turned in his chair and stared at the live oak just outside the office window. "I can't help but think you have an ulterior motive here, Scarlett. You're asking me to trust you, but—"

"Please, Joe. I owe you one. And I owe Dickie."

Lauren drove Joe to the Fort Lauderdale Airport. He kept his word with Scarlett, but there was more to it. He didn't want Lauren to worry. She was already a bit jumpy, for obvious reasons. Although, at the same time, maybe a bit hardened.

"I don't know why you won't tell me where you're going," Lauren said as she pulled up at passenger departure.

Joe looked out the window at the entrance to the airport. He turned to her. "I'll call you later today, let you know what it's all about. For now, I don't want you to worry."

"Is it a case?" she said. "Can you at least tell me *that*?"

"I'll tell you everything. When I call." He leaned over and gave her a kiss, but she wrapped her arms around him and pulled him close.

"Be careful," she said, then let go of him and wiped a tear from her cheek.

Joe forced a smile and stared back at her, still

unsure what the two of them were doing. Or what *he* was doing or what he was walking into by going to see Scarlett. He would have loved to have told Lauren more, but it was for her own good. No sense putting her in any more danger than she'd already experienced.

Joe stepped out from the car, then stuck his head inside keeping his hand on the door. "I'll call you as soon as I can." He closed the door and walked to the rear of Lauren's car. He opened the trunk and pulled out a travel bag and the locked hard-shell Pelican case he picked up from Juan for the Colt. He has little interest in using guns anymore, but he knew it'd be foolish going out there without one. He slammed the lid and walked toward the airport's entrance without turning back to give Lauren another look.

It was a little after ten thirty in the morning when Joe arrived at the Asheville Regional Airport. He walked through the gate and headed for baggage claim. He retrieved his gun from the baggage office.

By the time he got outside, the car Scarlett had promised was waiting for him. The man stood just outside with a black suit, no driver's cap, and a sign that had SHELDON printed in black marker across it.

The man reached for Joe's travel bag and the hard-shell case, but Joe pulled them back out of his reach. "Thanks, but I'll hold on to these."

The man opened the back passenger door.

Joe ducked his head inside and looked around, somewhat hesitant to step inside. But he got in.

The driver closed the door behind him and walked around the rear of the car, stepped inside and pulled from the curb and onto Terminal Drive toward Route 26.

Joe picked the case up from the floor and placed it on his lap. He removed the Colt, unlocked his travel bag and removed a box of bullets. He loaded the Colt and held on to it, resting it on his thigh. He looked up and caught the driver's eyes on him through the rearview mirror up front.

The driver glanced over his shoulder at Joe. "I'd prefer you don't have your weapon out like that, unless you're planning to shoot me?"

Joe assumed the man was making light of it. He cracked a slight smile. "I'm not interested in shooting anybody. But I do prefer to have it on me when I'm not sure what the hell I'm walking into."

The man turned his head and faced the road, but his eyes were back on the rearview mirror. He drove north on 26 past Biltmore Park and continued onto 74 until they hit 19 and continued north.

"Would you mind telling me where you're taking me?" Joe said.

The driver looked into the rearview at Joe. "Did you eat breakfast?"

"Does a vodka cranberry on the flight over

count?"

The driver smiled. "I'm taking you to Waffle House. That's all I was told to do."

Joe laughed but then realized the guy wasn't joking. "Waffle House? For real?"

The driver nodded. "I don't ask questions." He turned off Smokey Park Highway and into the Waffle House parking lot. He stopped at the front of the building, a few steps from the door.

Although Joe was sure he was the only person dropped off at the door of the Waffle House by a professional driver, he wasn't the only one in a Lincoln Town Car. The lot wasn't exactly full, but the parked cars were either similar in make to the Lincoln or pickup trucks.

The driver stepped out of the car and walked around to Joe's door. He pulled it open.

Joe stepped out and tucked the Colt in his pants. He reached into his pocket and tried to hand the man a couple of bills. "Thanks for the ride, I guess?"

But the man put his hands up. "No, sir. Can't accept that. Ms. Corban took care of everything."

"Who?"

"Ms. Corban. She'll be here soon." The driver walked around the front of the car and ducked inside, closed the door and drove off.

Joe stood on the sidewalk in front of the Waffle House with his bag over his shoulder and the empty hard-shell case in his hand. He watched the Lincoln pull out onto the Smokey Park Highway and disappear around the corner.

37

JOE SAT IN the booth at the back of the Waffle House and looked at his watch. It had been nearly thirty minutes since the driver had dropped him off. And he began to wonder exactly what was going on.

He had a feeling he didn't like and purposely chose the booth at the back on account of the stories he'd not only read, but written, about mob hits in places just like the Waffle House. There was the story his boss and mentor, Teddy Parsons, covered for the *Post* in 1967, when Thomas "The Enforcer" Altamura ate steak on Halloween night at A Place for Steak. Big Tony Esperti burst through the door and pumped five slugs into Altamura.

He couldn't picture Scarlett coming in to take him out. But he had no idea if she'd be alone.

He looked around at the crowd inside the place: mostly old people, the ones driving the big American cars out in the parking lot, and a handful of truck-driver types eating at the counter.

The front door opened. He watched a woman walk in from outside wearing dark sunglasses and a long sweater that went halfway down her thighs, over her jeans.

Joe watched her. He knew that familiar walk. She did a good job changing her look. Especially the short, black hair. But her walk, a little overconfident, was what gave her away.

She continued toward Joe and pulled her shades from her eyes and looked at him over the top of them.

He put his travel bag next to him, the Colt hidden underneath.

Scarlett kept her glasses on her face and sat across from Joe. She smiled and looked around. "You ever been to a Waffle House before? You don't look the type."

Joe didn't answer. "You look different."

She gave a slight shrug. "I'm a wanted woman." She looked toward the other tables, then put her finger up and gestured for the waitress. She pulled off her sunglasses. "Can I get a coffee, please?"

The waitress walked over to the table and looked at Joe. "Would you like me to warm up your cup?"

Joe pushed it toward the edge of the table. "Please."

"Would either of you like to order something to eat?"

"I'd just like a coffee," Scarlett said. "Maybe my

friend would like something?" She gave him a somewhat devious smile. "It's my treat."

He didn't like that. He said no to the waitress, and when she walked away, he said, "You mean *Dickie's* treat?"

The smile left Scarlett's face.

Joe said, "This is a long way for me to come for coffee at the Waffle House."

"I appreciate you coming." She turned and looked toward the door. "I'm glad you didn't call the cops."

He sipped his coffee and stared back at her.

She said, "I hope Mike took good care of you?"

"Mike? The driver?"

"We don't use our own cars around here, of course. And when you can afford to have someone else drive you around…"

"He called you Ms. Corban? I assume he doesn't know your real name?"

"You like that?" She flashed another smile. "I'm not as dumb as you think, Joe."

"I never said you were."

Scarlett turned and again looked over her shoulder in the direction of the entrance. "It's a lot grayer and cooler out here." She smiled as the waitress dropped off her cup of coffee and topped off Joe's cup. Once the waitress walked away, she said, "I do miss Miami."

Joe pushed the cup aside and leaned with his arms on the table, folded under him. "Whenever you're ready to start talking, I'm all ears," he said. He eyed the entrance. "I just hope there's not an unexpected surprise waiting for me outside."

She looked around at the thin crowd still in the restaurant, but most of the tables around them were empty. She held both hands tight around her coffee cup. "If it weren't for me, you'd already be dead. My sisters both thought it would be best for everyone if you were out of the picture."

Joe said, "Is that why I'm here?"

"So I can kill you?" Scarlett shook her head. "No."

"Then, why *am* I here? You're two hundred grand richer, assuming the three of you split it evenly. Isn't that what you were after?"

Scarlett looked into her cup. "If it was all about having money, I could've just stayed with Dickie. I had everything I needed. I had no reason to take his money."

"But if you never loved him or cared about him the way he did about you, then I can't imagine it would be all that much fun. And although he doesn't look the picture of health, you and I both know Dickie's one of those men who'll live forever. Maybe something you had to consider."

"I never said I didn't care about him the way he cares about me, did I?"

Joe stared back at Scarlett. "Well, when you tried to get me to—"

"I'm sorry about all of that," she said. She shrugged. "But you're an attractive man, Joe. Just because I…" She paused a moment. "It doesn't change the way I feel about Dickie."

Joe rolled his eyes and picked up his coffee. He took a sip and kept his eyes on her from over the rim. After a moment of silence, he said, "I'd appreciate it if you'd stop beating around the bush and tell me how this is going to work."

Scarlett nodded. "We're going to get Dickie his money back. Most of it, at least. I don't expect he'd ever take me back or we'll ever be together again, but—"

"You went through all this trouble? And now you feel guilty because, what, you're afraid karma's going to come back to bite you?"

Scarlett shook her head. "I told you, I'm innocent in all of this. My sisters, both of them, it was their idea. I was out with Matt when I met Dickie, but we weren't together. Not anymore. I knew Matt and Morgan were fooling around, but I didn't care. Not in the least. But when Matt saw me talking to Dickie, he got his friends involved."

"Idél and Eugene?"

"Yes, and it just so happens Eugene knew my other sister, Dawn."

"The whole gang got you to hook up with Dickie?" Joe said.

"The thing is," she said, "Dickie and Matt never met face-to-face. And when he saw Dickie that night at the bar, he already owed him some money. I guess he just thought if he didn't get to Dickie first

—"

"Dickie would have gone after him," Joe said.

Scarlett picked up her cup to take a sip but set it back down. "Idél was what you might call the mastermind. He put it all together. But I knew how much money Dickie had. At least I thought I did. And I knew once we split the pot, there wouldn't be enough to go around for all of us."

"So you and your sisters stuck to the plan, but cut Idél and Eugene out of it?"

She nodded. "Matt got caught in the middle."

Joe thought for a moment. "Wait a minute. Didn't you just try to tell me you didn't have anything to do with it?"

"Joe, the kidnapping was real. Once Idél figured out we were going to cut him out, he decided to push up the timeline. I wasn't expecting it when he took me. They blindfolded me, threw me in the back of a van, and—"

Joe scratched his head and looked out toward the other tables. "How'd you know they threw you in the back of a van if you were blindfolded?"

She stared back at him, her mouth slightly open, but words didn't come out. "Matt helped me escape. That's why Idél shot him."

Joe took a deep breath and closed his eyes. He rubbed his face with both hands and knew the caffeine wasn't doing nearly enough to wake him up. He looked at his watch. "I'd love to believe your story. But here you are hiding out in the mountains, got your own personal driver and—"

"Was I supposed to stick around, send my own sisters to prison?"

Joe stared back at her but didn't answer.

"But you helped get the money from Dickie before Idél went to meet him. And you threw your boyfriend Matt to the wolves in the process."

"He wasn't my boyfriend."

"But you got him killed, knowing he'd hold things up while Idél was at the house trying to shake down Dickie, because he assumed Dickie decided not to show up with the money."

Scarlett looked into her coffee, then raised her eyes to Joe. "I didn't think Idél would go after Dickie like he did."

Joe laughed. "You'd have to be pretty naïve to think he wouldn't." He narrowed his eyes and stared back at Scarlett. "You're lucky he didn't get killed."

Scarlett closed her eyes for a moment. "I had no choice."

"No choice? How about warning Dickie, telling him what was about to go down, while you still had the chance?"

The waitress walked up to their table and filled both their cups with more coffee. "You sure you don't want to order something to eat?"

Joe and Scarlett both shook their heads, although Joe was getting hungry.

The waitress turned and walked away.

"So, now you want to give Dickie his money

back?"

Scarlett took a moment before she answered, looking across at Joe. "At least what's left of it."

38

JOE STOPPED THE Ford Explorer Scarlett had rented for him and looked at the number on the mailbox at the bottom of the steep, dirt driveway. He turned the wheel and drove slow up the hill for a good twenty yards or so. The gravel popped and crunched under the tires. As soon as he saw a piece of the white ranch house through the thick evergreens, he pulled the Explorer off to the edge of the driveway and parked between the trees.

He stepped out, careful as he pushed the door closed, trying to not make much noise. He tossed the empty duffel bag over his shoulder and walked a few yards in the woods, but stayed along the driveway. He had the Colt 1911 in his hand, down by his side.

He moved from tree to tree and ducked behind a row of evergreen shrubs when he got closer to the house. He saw a Mercedes and an old Chevy S-10 pickup truck parked in front of the long, one-level ranch. He eyed the barn-like structure Scarlett had mentioned was behind the house at the edge of the woods.

Joe breathed in the cool mountain air. He liked it more than the thick humidity that filled his lungs throughout the year in Miami, although he didn't like the cold and knew that would be the part that would be hard to handle if he ever decided to live out in the mountains one day.

He stayed low and walked across the driveway, crouched down behind the Mercedes and truck until he could see the wrap-around deck that started on the side of the house and went around to the back. It overlooked a huge yard, almost the length and width of two football fields. He walked back toward the truck and noticed an old wood stock shotgun resting in a gun rack on the back window. He tried the passenger-side door and pulled it open.

Nice thing about living out in the country; you don't always have to lock your car doors.

He reached inside and grabbed the gun. He looked it over, wasn't even sure it worked. But he didn't mind having it as backup or for the look he thought might work a little better.

He tucked the Colt in his pants and held the shotgun's barrel pointed toward the ground. He continued around the back of the barn and watched the house from the side along the woods. He looked for movement inside the house but couldn't see anyone. He stayed low and moved closer, got up to the side of the house and ducked under one of the windows. He looked out toward the front of the house, then out into the back.

Everything seemed so quiet. Something he wasn't exactly used to.

He slowly straightened out under the window and peeked inside over the sill. He looked down a hall and into the kitchen where one of the sisters sat at an island with a drink in her hand. He wasn't sure which sister it was, with her back to where he stood.

He walked along the house and looked in through another window. This time, with a better view he could see it was Dawn seated at the island. But she wasn't alone. Morgan sat across from her, a bottle of wine between them.

He didn't see Scarlett inside but she was very precise with the plan they discussed at the Waffle House. He knew exactly where she'd be.

Joe walked around to the back of the house. And as soon as he turned the corner, he saw her seated in a lounge chair soaking up the sun. Or so she was supposed to be.

Scarlett had her back to him, but she glanced at him over her shoulder and acted as if he wasn't there.

Joe reached into his back pocket and pulled out the ski mask. He slipped it onto his head and pulled it over his face. He pumped the rack on the shotgun and Scarlett screamed. She jumped from the lounge chair and he grabbed her, locked his arm around her neck.

He walked her to the sliding glass doors and looked into the kitchen. Neither sister seemed to be paying much attention. Joe whispered into Scarlett's ear, "You might need to scream a little louder."

So she did. And both sisters turned toward Joe and Scarlett with their eyes wide open.

Scarlett screamed again. "Help! Help me!"

Joe pulled her back from the door, practically dragging her feet underneath her.

"You're hurting me," she screamed.

Joe looked straight at Morgan and her sister through the glass with the shotgun in his hand. "I want the money. All of it! Or Scarlett dies!" He wished he'd thought of something better to say. He'd rehearsed a few things in his head on the ride over.

But they got the point.

He backed away from the door without taking his eyes off the sisters through the glass. He dragged Scarlett with him.

The two sisters stood frozen, although the sun had a slight shift and created a reflection on the glass, making it harder to see inside.

But he could see them clear enough. "Get out here. Now!" he yelled.

Scarlett screamed her sisters' names. "Morgan! Dawn! Help me! Please! Do what he says! He'll kill me!"

Joe yelled, "You have thirty seconds to get out here with the money!"

But the way they both stared back at him through the glass—frozen in place without either saying a word—made Joe wonder if they could hear him at all. It didn't make sense. He lifted the barrel of the shotgun and pointed it up toward Scarlett's head. He whispered to her out of the corner of his mouth. "What the hell are they doing in there?"

He shifted Scarlett behind him and switched hands with his gun, but kept it pressed against the back of her head, somewhere below her ear. He reached for the handle on the sliding glass door and slid it open. There was nothing between them.

He backed away from the open door and stared at Dawn. He wanted to yell he knew she killed Will. But it wouldn't be worth blowing his cover.

"I want the money you took from Dickie. All six hundred grand."

He couldn't understand why they looked so calm. Maybe they were stoned. Both still stood there, staring out at Joe and Scarlett without a word.

Scarlett screamed, "What are you doing in there? He's going to kill me if you don't do what he says! Please, help me!"

Morgan put her hands in the air and stepped toward the door. "Okay, okay. Listen, don't hurt her. She hasn't done a thing. But I don't know what you're talking about. Who's Dickie?"

Scarlett's hair was pressed up against Joe's chin,

and he tried to look down at her. He couldn't ask if Morgan was being serious or not, but that's what he wondered.

Dawn yelled, "Don't hurt her! We'll give you whatever you want."

Morgan turned and looked at her. "But we don't know what he's talking about. Right?"

"Don't bullshit me, ladies. I know exactly what's going on." Joe took his eyes off the two for a brief second.

But it was long enough for Dawn to lift her hand with a gun she'd pulled from a purse on the island in front of her. She fired a shot at Joe.

And out of instinct, he turned. But when he did, he exposed Scarlett.

She screamed and he knew the bullet struck her. Her legs gave out from under her.

Joe eased Scarlett to the floor of the deck, and Dawn fired another shot. But Joe was ready and had lifted the shotgun toward the house. He pulled the trigger, and the glass on the door exploded. The shot wasn't even close. He pulled the trigger again, but of course nothing happened.

The sister yelled from inside, "You think we're stupid, Scarlett?"

Joe dropped the shotgun and helped Scarlett to her feet and got her around to the side of the house, out of the way. "Shit," he said as he helped her down into a seated position and leaned her up against the clapboards. He kneeled in front of her and looked at her shirt, where the blood had soaked through.

She looked him in the eye. "I'm okay," she said and followed it with a cough.

Joe stepped around the corner with his Colt out in front of him. He pointed it at Morgan but didn't know where the other sister was. "She needs an ambulance," he said.

Morgan pointed toward the barn. "The money's in there. Up the ladder." She had her hands raised. "You can take the mask off, Joe." She turned and looked behind her, and Dawn walked out of the house with a shotgun of her own. She fired and Joe ducked, then jumped off the side of the deck and hid underneath. "Your sister's going to die if you don't get her to a doctor," he yelled through the deck boards.

He heard Dawn scream at Morgan, "Why'd you tell him?"

He saw a shadow moving toward him through the slits in the decking, then stepped out and pointed the Colt up toward Dawn. "I should shoot you right now, for killing Will."

She turned and ran back into the house and of course Joe didn't fire, even though he could have shot her right in the back.

He looked over at Scarlett with Morgan crouched in front of her. Without another thought he ran for the barn. He pulled on the door, but it was locked. He lifted the Colt and fired three shots, blew the lock clean off the door. He pulled it open and hurried inside. The doors closed behind him.

It was dark and stank of mildew. He walked past the riding mower and the rakes and shovels leaning up against the wall. He looked side to side, then saw the wooden ladder, tucked the Colt into his pants and ran for it. But as soon as he stepped onto the first rung, sunlight broke into the barn.

The double doors swung open and Dawn stepped inside with the shotgun. She pumped and fired at Joe, blew a hole the size of a baseball through the side of the barn.

Joe jumped from the ladder and ducked behind the lawnmower. He watched her trying to reload but wasn't about to give her the time she would've needed. He grabbed an old rusty shovel with a wooden handle and ran toward her, swung it at the shotgun and knocked it out of her hands.

She turned to run but tripped over the threshold and screamed as she fell hard onto the wooden ramp just outside the barn door. She grabbed her ankle and Joe stood over her, the Colt pointed at her face.

She looked up at him from the floor of the barn. "I thought it was you I'd shot that morning."

Joe stared back at her, confused for a split second. But then it hit him. She'd killed Will, but the bullet was meant for himself.

He turned from her and jumped on the ladder, climbed up and into the loft. He spotted the same suitcase Dickie'd delivered the money in and grabbed on to it. He tossed it off the side to the barn's floor, then climbed down the ladder and picked it up.

Dawn looked to be in pain, still holding her ankle with both hands. "You didn't even have the balls to shoot me."

Joe gave her a slight smile. "Don't tempt me." He walked past her and out toward the driveway. He gave Morgan a nod. "You call the rescue?"

She nodded. "They're on the way."

He held up the briefcase. "I know this can't be easy." He continued across the driveway toward the Explorer, then looked back at the three sisters. "I hear Waffle House is hiring."

Dickie was by himself at the bar at Mickey Cho's with a plate of jumbo shrimp and a sushi roll of some sort in front of him.

Joe walked up behind him, sat on the open stool next to him and watched Dickie finish what was in his mouth.

Dickie wiped his hands with the napkin from his lap, then wiped his mouth. He smiled and slid the plate of shrimp toward Joe. "You hungry, Joey?"

Joe looked down at the plate but shook his head. He waved over to the bartender and ordered a vodka cranberry.

Dickie nodded toward his glass. "You drink a lot

of that cranberry juice. Must never have any problems with your pee, huh?"

Joe gave him a funny look, but it wasn't the first time Dickie had said it.

Dickie sipped his martini, then turned and looked back over his shoulder. "Where's Lauren?"

"She actually decided not to come. She's going out of town for a job interview."

"Out of town, huh? What's that mean, she'd move out of Miami?"

Joe shrugged. "I'm not sure. I guess so. We didn't spend much time talking after I got back."

Dickie smiled. "Ohhh, okay. I get it."

Joe shook his head and sipped his vodka cranberry. "No, I don't mean that. It's just... she was getting prepared for the trip. And I had some things I had to take care of."

Dickie said, "I thought you two were going to stick together. You make a nice couple."

Joe hesitated a moment, wasn't sure how much he wanted to go into his personal life with Dickie. But he realized they were actually friends. Maybe more than he wanted to admit. "We've decided to pull back on that for a bit. Neither one of us is looking for a relationship, I guess."

Dickie made a face. "What's that supposed to mean? If you both like each other, then..."

Joe stared across the bar toward the back of the restaurant, looking out at Biscayne Bay.

Dickie said, "But don't you get lonely? Being

alone all the time?"

Joe hadn't really ever thought about it like that. He let out a slight laugh. "I don't know. Not really."

Dickie looked into his martini glass, picked up a shrimp but put it back on his plate. "I don't like being alone," he said. He turned and looked at Joe. "I miss her, you know." He looked away, then back to Joe. "I'd give up every dime I have." He shook his head. "Money's not everything." But then he lifted his glass and raised it to Joe. "But it doesn't hurt to have it either." He looked toward the door when two middle-aged women walked into the bar.

Joe watched them, too, as they pulled up a stool at the far end from where Joe and Dickie sat.

Dickie shrugged and looked back at Joe and raised his glass once again. "And you know what?" He nodded once. "There's plenty of fish in the sea."

If you enjoyed *Play It Cool*, please share your thoughts with others by leaving a review with the store where you purchased it. It would mean a lot to me as an author and to others interested in learning what readers like you think about the book. Thank you!

Please Join My Reader's List

Sign-up to receive free stories, giveaways, and VIP announcements when new books are released. When you do, you'll receive two free books, *Tell Them I'm Dead* and *What Have You Done?*

Visit **GregoryPayette.com/free-book** to sign up.

Books by Gregory Payette

Stand Alone Crime Fiction

Tell Them I'm Dead

Cross Road (Henry Walsh Prequel)

Drag the Man Down

Half Cocked

Danny Womack's .38

Play It Cool (Joe Sheldon)

Play It Again (Joe Sheldon, Fall 2021)

The Henry Walsh Series

Henry Walsh Series Book 1: Dead at Third

Henry Walsh Series Book 2: The Last Ride

Henry Walsh Series Book 3: The Crystal Pelican

Henry Walsh Series Book 4: The Night the Music Died

Henry Walsh Series Book 5: Dead Men Don't Smile

Henry Walsh Series Book 6: Dead in the Creek

Henry Walsh Series Book 7: Dropped Dead

Learn more by visiting GregoryPayette.com

Made in the USA
Middletown, DE
27 May 2021